IAN PURDIE

PYRAMID
ASIA

For Bagurkle Rinpoche.

iii

Other books by Ian Purdie:
The Imnothero Principle
Splatterpuss
The Book of Nasty

CONTENTS

PRELUDE

A blur of fur passed in front of the two boys.

"Was that a rat?"

"Too many legs."

It was hot and there wasn't enough oxygen in the air. The barren mountainside had lost a lot of its allure since the snow melted. The higher they climbed, the closer they got to the sun.

Wen and Tashi had always known that one day they would climb the mountain which loomed over their childhoods, dwarfing the small Tibetan village of Womadige.

They grew up hearing stories about the demons and other-worldly apparitions that haunted its upper slopes. They watched it change with the seasons, sometimes showing a new face every minute as its mighty bulk continually transformed before their young eyes.

Now it was under their feet, adorning their pre-adolescent sky like a pert young breast.

Upwards it dared them.

After more sweat, heat, dust, rocks and going upwards than either had imagined they were committed to or capable of, they rested on a ledge just below the significantly less looming summit.

The view was spectacular. They could see almost everything they'd ever known at a glance, and there was so much more.

The river their mothers had washed their clothes in since they were babies meandered off into the distance in two opposing directions.

Far below, their homes were barely visible.

"Let's go," said Tashi.

Upwards.

Clinging precariously to a cliff in front of Tashi was an insignificant, undernourished botanical growth. Not quite a mountain shrub, it had been born from the anus of a passing eagle and had splattered onto the side of the mountain, germinating in the cruel sun of a particularly hot summer. It clung to an embedded boulder, enduring one of the harshest environments on Earth.

The boulder proved to be stable right up until the moment Tashi grabbed hold of the plant, attempting to drag himself upwards. His weight was enough to bring the plant, the boulder, and both the boys crashing back down onto the ledge below, in a hail of dirt.

"What's that?" asked Wen, dusting himself off and pointing to an odd shaped rock that had bounced off Tashi's head.

"What's what?" asked Tashi less interested in the object than the damage it might have done.

It was clearly different to everything else surrounding it.

Wen picked it up.

"It looks like some kind of ornament."

"Let me have a look," said Tashi.

Then Wen saw something else in the debris.

"Here's another one! What do you think they are?"

"I don't know," replied Tashi, still examining the first object. "Something pretty hard."

"They look like they might fit together. They're made out of the same stuff," said Wen.

Neither of them recognised the material. It wasn't rock, brick, plaster or plastic.

"This one looks like it's got some kind of strange writing on it."

"This one does too," said Wen.

"I wonder where they came from."

Tashi fitted the objects together to form a miniature pyramid.

"I wonder how it got up here," said Wen.

"Are there any more pieces?" asked Tashi.

"I can't see any."

Tashi separated the two parts and they each stuffed one half of the ornament into their shirts before continuing their upward ascent. After another half hour, Wen climbed triumphantly onto the flat mesa-like pinnacle of Mt Luguna.

They were on top of the world. Snow covered peaks spiked the horizon in every direction. As the sun completed its journey towards the blue haze of distant mountains, the final rays lit up a series of ephemeral pyramids in the thin clouds.

ONE - THE MERCIFUL PART

Chapter one should not be confused with chapter won. Nobody won.

Wen was the one who lost the most. He died. And that was the merciful part; merciful to his mother and everybody else who had helplessly witnessed his tragic decline.

Wen became a drug addict. He started using heroin at the age of 15, just after his second step-father began beating him.

It was then he moved away from his mother and started living with Jim.

Jim was 17 years older than Wen but he wasn't a great role model. Jim taught Wen everything he didn't need to know. On everything from mixing up a hit, to lubricating a sex toy, Jim was a veritable encyclopedia.

An ex-pat Australian, Jim had managed to offend, in equal measure, both sides of the law in his native jurisdiction. Australia was a broad minded country, but Jim had pushed the limits of tolerance even in such an easy going place.

He was wanted by both the Australian Federal Police and the Comanchero motorcycle gang for his involvement in crimes and misdemeanours too numerous to elaborate, here.

A 'friend' inside the Australian Federal Police had tipped him off that he was under surveillance, more than enough incentive for him to rip off his associates in the Comanchero's and plan an untimely exit. Their control of the lucrative Sydney ecstasy and meth-amphetamine trades had made them a wealthy, worthy target.

Jim narrowly avoided a Comanchero bullet and a police sting and boarded a 747 bound for Katmandu with a suitcase stuffed full of cash.

Besides this one piece of luggage, he had only the clothes he'd worn to the airport.

However, once safely out of Australia, the $3.7 million in his suitcase allowed him to bribe his way through

Kathmandu airport, and then, having purchased a new wardrobe and acquired suitable travel documents, bribe his way into Tibet. There he was able to set himself up in relative luxury, if you don't mind yak dung. The local authorities were happy to ignore his lack of a visa for a regular fee that was always paid on time, in cash and with a generous bonus.

Wen was formally welcomed onto the campus of junkie university late one night with a black eye and bruised ribs administered by his step father. Arriving injured and in need of immediate medication, under the expert tuition of Professor Jim he was destined to become a leading researcher in the fertile field of auto-intoxication.

Wen's discovery of Scotch whiskey completed the trinity of self abuse that separates the fully optioned deviate from the mere self abuser. Despite the isolated location, Jim had organised for a case of Glenfiddich to mysteriously arrive every month and it was a natural progression that Wen should become a participant in its not so mysterious disappearance.

Bisexuality, drug addiction and alcoholism constitute the three immutable pillars absolutely crucial to sustain this rare and delicate life form.

So it was an immense tragedy when a still smouldering joint dropped onto an open copy of Tom Robbin's *Jitterbug Perfume*, resulting in a fire that burnt Jim's house down, with him and Wen unconscious in the middle of it. The world lost two fully optioned deviates in less than ten minutes, proving once again, what fragile creatures these people are.

Tashi did much better.

When he was seven-years-old, his parents took him to Lhasa. For them the trip was a pilgrimage to the Buddhist Sera Monastery. For Tashi it was the first time he saw real members of the distantly despised Chinese community. They drove past in large, shiny cars, the men dressed in dark, tailored suits and the women in fine silks.

He'd heard a lot of bad things about the Chinese from his fellow villagers, but when he compared them to the rural peasant community he'd been brought up in, he decided he'd rather be Chinese.

They were clean and appeared to live superior lives of opulence and prosperity. They laughed and seemed a lot happier than the average Tibetan.

After the family returned to Womadige, Tashi was determined to learn to speak Chinese. He applied himself scrupulously to his studies and was the top pupil in his year at the school in nearby Nagqu.

Eventually his diligence paid off and he was awarded a rare scholarship by the central government in Beijing to study at a Chinese university, one that didn't supply free syringes and KY jelly.

He enrolled at the Institute of Tibetan Nationalities in Xian'yang, a small city, 23 kilometres from historic Xi'an.

He decided to study dentistry, a practical profession he hoped would allow him to live like the Chinese while also being able to help his fellow villagers.

The scholarship was a great deposit but wouldn't fully cover his expenses. Even if his entire village donated their year's earnings to help pay for his education, it wouldn't have been enough. But his choice of the unpopular but worthy career of dentistry helped him to secure a loan from the Chinese Agricultural Bank.

His mother cried as he boarded the train at Nagqu railway station to begin the 2,450 kilometre journey to Xi'an.

The 28 hours, travelling 'third class, hard seat', was an education in itself. During the journey he met several young Chinese and was able to converse with them, even though his clothing and accent set him apart.

The city of Xi'an was beyond anything he'd ever imagined. Modern and thriving, it represented everything he wanted his life to be. Crowds of beautifully dressed city dwellers swarmed in every direction. Cars and buses ferried the city's millions of inhabitants along wide, clean streets patrolled by traffic wardens and policemen in neat, crisp uniforms.

The final leg of his journey involved a train trip from Xi'an to Xian'yang. It was over in 18 minutes, another reflection of the fabulously fast pace of life he so desperately wanted to become a part of.

He carried his only bag filled with freshly washed, neatly ironed but threadbare clothes to the university campus and was directed to his dormitory by an efficient young clerk at the university's registration office.

* * *

Tashi and Ping met in the cafeteria. Ping usually avoided the cafeteria. She thought it was decadent and unhealthy, but on the day she met Tashi she had made an exception, and was in line behind him waiting to buy her lunch.

Ping thought Tashi was disgusting. In front of her in the queue, he chose fatty, sugary, over-processed poison on every possible occasion. He piled sugar onto anything that provided a suitable platform, showing as much respect for his teeth and insight into the concept of nutrition as a freshly poisoned goldfish.

By the time they arrived at the cashier Ping was lecturing Tashi on his diet and general health. She had him turned around and walking backwards. It was an encounter from which neither ever recovered.

Ping was studying archaeology, history, anthropology and the Tibetan language. She and Tashi were the most exotic combination of incongruous ingredients the cafeteria would ever facilitate mixing. But mix they did and the recipe produced a result far more agreeable to romantics than to mainstream academics or gourmets.

Love is an extremely complex subject, a composite, made up of many parts.

Part one is lust. Upon this platform, which eventually dissolves, a complicated edifice of trust, commitment, admiration, adoration, and empathy is painstakingly constructed.

Love needs a future. Without a future, love quickly morphs into misery and despair. It grows fangs and eats away at its victim's heart.

Love is dangerous, but try telling that to teenagers.

Ping paid cash, Tashi had a food voucher. They continued to debate the dangers of modern dietary trends as they sat together at one of the long benches filling the crowded, noisy dining hall.

The next subject was Tashi's table manners. He didn't have any according to Ping, who considered most mainlanders devoid of the most rudimentary etiquette.

She was from Hong Kong where, she assured him, nobody burped or spat, or shoveled food into their mouths like they were throwing logs into a furnace.

Tashi was fascinated. The concept of table manners was as alien to him as flying saucers. In fact any kind of saucers were far more sophisticated than anything he'd ever experienced in Womadige.

After augmenting each other's education way beyond any aspects of the official curriculum, they reluctantly parted and headed to opposite ends of the campus to immerse their minds in subjects that were closer to opposite than intellectual endeavors normally accommodate.

Tashi lived in one of the university dormitories with seven other male students. He slept in a bunk, the second up from the bottom with two others above him and another four bunks on the other side of the room. The rules were very strict with a rigidly enforced 11pm curfew. Girls were only allowed in the boys' dormitories during Tibetan New Year and otherwise they were similarly confined to their own dormitories.

China's one child policy insisted that potential parents first be married. Interaction between the sexes at this extremely volatile stage of their development was actively discouraged.

But it was too late for Tashi and Ping. They were busy constructing a composite of blissful togetherness based on a strong foundation of never mentioned, never acknowledged and never demonstrated lust.

Ping's father was a wealthy Hong Kong businessman and was worth more than every yak in Tibet.

Ping rented a small flat near the university campus. The first time she took him home, Tashi thought she was playing some kind of trick on him. It was more opulent than anywhere he'd ever been in his life. He'd finally attained his briefly glimpsed, childhood vision of nirvana.

After about two months the inevitable happened. Ping began talking about her family in terms that strongly implied Tashi would soon be meeting them. Tashi hoped this meant they would be coming to the mainland. It didn't. It meant he was going to Hong Kong. Apparently the break after the next semester was the most convenient time for her busy father.

Inevitability doesn't budge, it doesn't negotiate. Inevitability is fascist, dogmatic certainty, cleverly disguised as fascist, dogmatic certainty. Inevitability doesn't need to hide.

Nor did Tashi. He accepted inevitability and bowed graciously to 'the will of the family'.

This introduced a whole new series of never before imagined problems. Ping expected to fly to Hong Kong and she expected Tashi to fly with her so they would arrive together, at face value a reasonable expectation. However it also assumed a financial capacity that was not within the range of Tashi's otherwise impressive arsenal of abilities. With his family's help he hoped it might be marginally less improbable.

He phoned home, in itself a major organisational undertaking. Nobody in or near Womadige possessed a device anything like a telephone. It required Tashi to write his parents a letter, requesting they be at the Nagqu post office at a specific time so they could take the call. It took a week to arrange.

Ping had a cell phone and took less than five seconds to punch in the numbers Tashi provided.

"Hello?"

"Tashi! Is that you?"

"Hello mother."

"What's the matter? Why are you telephoning us?"

"I want to speak with dad."

"Are you in trouble?"

"No I'm not. Quite the opposite."

"Somebody else is in trouble? One of your friends?"

"Nobody's in trouble mum. Can I speak to dad?"

"Not unless you tell me what's wrong."

"Nothing is wrong mum. Everything is fine. I just need to talk to dad that's all."

"Are you sure?"

"Yes of course I'm sure. Is dad there?"

"Wait a minute."

"Hello Tashi. Is that you?"

"Hello dad."

"What's the matter. Your mother said one of your friends is in trouble."

"Nobody's in trouble."

"Well why are you spending money on a long distance telephone call?"

"I need some money."

"What for?"

"I have to go to Hong Kong."

"What?"

"I've met a girl and I want to go and meet her family."

"In Hong Kong?"

"That's right. I need to borrow some money to pay for the airfare."

"Airfare?"

"Yes. We want to fly."

"Fly?"

"We don't have enough time to travel over land."

"I need to talk to your mother. Wait."

The rest of the conversation didn't go so well. When Tashi's mother re-entered the conversation, all his remaining hope ran for its life.

Money had never been one of the blessings enjoyed by Tashi's family. Instead they had been blessed with long hours of thankless labor and very little to show for it. They were blessed with each other and they were blessed by the fact that some of the seasons were less harsh than others.

Having their son phone wanting money was less of a blessing than a day with no wind. It was like being blessed by a dying leper.

Anything but money would have been fine. They could have given him a whole sack of turnips, several chickens or even a new born kitten, but money? Money was something other people, rich people had.

Tashi terminated the call.

He was poor.

His parents were poor.

His parent's parents were poor. It was in their genes. They had been endowed with genetic poverty. There wasn't much else they could be proud of except their turnips and their neat but threadbare clothes.

Tashi knew he had a deep well of pride inside somewhere, but none of it was of the slightest use to him when Ping took back her cell phone and asked how the call had gone.

Money was something you couldn't bluff. When the bill arrived you needed to pay. Any other outcome was exactly where he was at, as Ping waited expectantly for his answer.

There is more to life than less. There is also the truth.

"I'm poor," he said. "I can't afford to fly to Hong Kong. I can barely afford to walk there. My shoes wouldn't make it, even if I mailed them."

Ping laughed.

TWO - WELCOME TO HONG KONG

Ping's mother stood beside her father, like a delicately scented flower growing beside a gravel pit. Ping's father looked like he'd had a bad day. Sweat filled the wrinkles on his brow as he contorted his unwelcoming features into something most smiles would be afraid of.

"Welcome to Hong Kong," he said extending a paw designed to crush walnuts.

"Hello, thank you," said Tashi, surrendering his small, innocent appendage into the patriarch's formidable grip.

"So lovely to meet you," said Ping's mother after she and Ping had finished hugging and kissing each other. Her smile was warm and she appeared to be teetering unsurely on the verge of another embrace before checking herself and resuming her place beside the gravel pit.

An anonymous little man in a black suit scampered about, silently insistent that he was going to carry their bags. Outside in the car park, a large black Mercedes swallowed them up. The driver piloted the formidable machine through the streets of a city even bigger and busier than Xi'an.

Ping's happy laughter filled the car as she brought her parents up to date with her scholastic progress and most recent purchases.

The car was ushered through an impressive wrought iron gate by two uniformed impressive wrought iron gate attendants.

The house was enormous. It formed the centre piece of an estate that could have fitted the entire Potala Palace comfortably into one small corner.

Somebody opened the car's doors and they climbed the front steps of the mansion into an entrance hall as vast and spacious as the lobby of a museum. Marble was its dominant feature, making it seem cold. There were many, no doubt spectacularly expensive vases overflowing with professionally arranged flowers. Modern art hung on white walls. Above it all was an enormous crystal chandelier.

A large staircase drew them upwards.

When they reached its summit they were ushered into another large room filled with furniture that seemed far too precious to sit on. Tashi did his best to make himself less uncomfortable, contributing as much as he could to a stunted conversation gasping for life above the room's intricately patterned rugs.

Tashi was certain he must be the poorest person ever to be allowed to set an ill-shod foot inside this temple of unbelievable opulence.

Then he noticed it.

On the wall behind his host and hostess perched an ornately framed oil painting. It depicted an object that Tashi recognised; an object he hadn't seen for many years, since he'd consigned half of it to a box stored in the roof of his parents' humble peasant dwelling back in the real world.

"What's that?" he asked, realising too late he'd interrupted Ping's father in mid-sentence.

Ping's father stopped speaking and turned to consider the subject of his daughter's young suitor's curiosity. An awkward silence, punctuated by the ticking of a large clock, wallowed in the freshly created void.

"It's a painting by a monk," Ping's mother interjected nervously as her mouth attempted to smile.

"That old thing?" asked Ping's father. "I got it at an auction on the mainland. It used to belong to the Governor of Amdo Province."

"That's where I come from. What's it supposed to be?"

"It's a pleasing shape," soothed Ping's mother.

"I think it's ugly," said Ping.

"I don't know," answered Ping's father. "I don't think it's supposed to be anything real. Why do you ask?"

"I find its shape interesting," said Tashi, attempting to emulate their nonchalance. "I'm sorry. I interrupted you."

Ping's father turned and readjusted his focus. The abandoned conversation was tactfully revived by Ping's mother.

The rest of the afternoon merged seamlessly into the evening and after what Tashi considered a banquet that could have fed his entire village for a month, he and Ping were escorted up another staircase and shown into two adjoining bedrooms.

Tashi entered a sumptuously appointed boudoir. It was the type of room he imagined an ancient Chinese emperor would have felt at home inside. The bed was ornately carved teak with silk and lace bed clothes. A large bay window afforded a panoramic view of Victoria Harbor dotted with the lights of more ships than he had ever seen in any book.

His bag looked like a souvenir from a garbage tip amongst the room's other contents. It had been placed on a velvet chair near the bed. Savouring the fact that he was alone for the first time since he'd left his dormitory that morning, Tashi fell backwards onto the bed, kicking off his sandals.

Just as his normal peasant persona was bravely reassembling itself amid the prosperity, the door swung inward. Ping entered the room. Her scent invaded him.

"I'm sorry about all that," she said, sitting on the bed beside him.

"All what?" he asked as if luxury was a normal feature of his life.

"You know, the Chinese, Tibetan thing. My parents like you, I could tell."

"What Chinese, Tibetan thing?" he asked, feigning cultural ignorance.

They both laughed.

"I couldn't help noticing your family photos. You didn't tell me you have an older brother," said Tashi.

"He died when I was sixteen," answered Ping. "He had a motorbike accident."

"I'm sorry."

"My father still hasn't forgiven himself for letting him buy a high powered bike. He smashed himself into an oncoming car."

After a furtive hug, Ping was gone.

Tashi was exhausted. It had been one of the most eventful days of his life. He felt very strange as he displaced the immaculate bedding and buried himself amongst it. Sleep arrived almost instantaneously, a complete waste of the settings he occupied.

Tashi incorporated the first thud into the dream he was having. It didn't really fit in with the wide open countryside and various chattels that were dominating his sleeping mind. The second thud woke him. The third thud was accompanied by the sound of wood splintering and was followed by footsteps that got louder until the bedroom door burst open. A bright light shone around the room before fixing itself blindingly onto him.

"What's happening?" he muttered feebly as several more lights flooded into the room. Then he became aware of the barrels of what appeared to be very sophisticated weaponry.

"Don't move!" commanded a gruff male voice.

"What's happening?" he repeated.

"Shut up!" commanded the voice.

"All clear!" barked another voice before some of the lights were redirected, illuminating the silhouettes of several men leaving the room.

"Get out of bed!" commanded the voice.

"Get out of bed now!" it commanded from behind three gun barrels.

"What do you want?"

A sharp pain erupted inside his head. It was the last thing he remembered before everything went dark black.

* * *

Ping was holding Tashi's hand. He was in bed in a room that smelled far cleaner than he was.

"Where am I?"

"You're in hospital," answered Ping, squeezing his hand.

"I'll leave you two alone," declared a female voice Tashi didn't recognise.

"This is my friend, Aixia."

"How's your head?" asked the beautiful young woman behind the unrecognised voice.

"Not very good. What happened?"

Ping was uncharacteristically silent. She averted her eyes.

"I'll leave you two alone," repeated Aixia, executing a tactical retreat.

Ping and Aixia had been friends 'since they were born', as they were fond of telling anybody who asked. They had no recollection of a first meeting and for both of them their relationship had simply always been. They attended St Clare's Girl's School together and had only been separated by Ping's decision to pursue a tertiary education on the mainland. Aixia's family weren't as affluent as Ping's and her choices of vocation weren't as expansive or expensive. She worked as a chemist's assistant.

"The police raided my father's house," Ping replied after Aixia had left the room.

"What? Why?"

"They arrested him and took him to the police station."

Tashi wondered what kind of strange universe he'd awoken into. It bore very little resemblance to the one he went to sleep in. Ping's eyes met his and she began to cry.

"I'm sorry," she sobbed. "I don't know why they did this to you."

"Don't worry," he tried to reassure her. "It must be a mistake. I'm sure everything will work out fine in the end. Where's your mother?"

"She's in another room. They had to sedate her. She was hysterical."

Tashi tried to sit up but his head exploded with pain.

"Don't try to move," said Ping. "They nearly broke your skull."

"I don't understand how this could have happened," he said feeling his bandaged head.

"They were looking for my father."

"Why?"

Ping turned away and began sobbing again.

"Don't cry," said Tashi. "I'm sure they'll sort it all out."

"They accused him of being a heroin smuggler."

"What?!"

"They said he was the leader of an international drug trafficking cartel."

"There has to be a mistake," said Tashi incredulously. "Your father wouldn't do anything like that! Would he?"

"Of course not. He's a businessman."

"What kind of businessman?"

"He's an exporter." Ping's answer merged with the throbbing pain in his head.

* * *

Tashi was discharged the next afternoon. His head was still bandaged and he felt dizzy every time he tried to stand up. He and Ping caught a taxi back to her father's house.

The police had deleted a lot of the mansion's former magnificence, dismembering several pieces of furniture and even ripping up some slaps of marble. Despite the best efforts of a veritable army of staff, it bore scant resemblance to the palace they'd been welcomed into three days earlier.

As they sat in the wreckage of the room they'd occupied with Ping's parents the day they arrived, Tashi's eyes strayed onto the painting that still hung defiantly in what was now a place of dishonour above the fireplace.

"Have you any idea what that's supposed to be?" he asked.

"You asked that the other day. Why do you care about an ugly old painting?"

"I found something that looks exactly like that thing in the picture when I was a boy climbing the mountain behind my village"

"Really?" said Ping suddenly interested. "Do you still have it?"

"It's at my parent's house. It had two parts and my friend who was with me when we found it, took the other half. They fitted together and formed a kind of pyramid, just like the one in the painting."

"That's very interesting," said Ping.

* * *

Ping's mother came home, became hysterical again and had to be sedated and re-admitted to hospital. Ping's father was charged with heroin trafficking and denied bail. They didn't see him again before they had to fly back to Xian'yang to continue their studies.

Otherwise there was Aixia. She was determined to inject some frivolity into the tragic mess her friend was being forced to endure. Most of her solution involved alcohol. The rest relied heavily on ad-lib declarations of undying love whilst intoxicated and giggled reminders of past transgressions, the exact nature of which Tashi was too frightened to attempt to guess.

Aixia was able to create the temporary illusion of being back in school, teenagers getting ready to go to a party. Everything was in front of them. Anything and everything that had nothing to do with heroin, police, drug couriers or jail cells.

THREE - THE ORACLE OF SINGH MA

The flight back to Xian'yang was very turbulent. Tashi was sure they weren't going to survive despite Ping's calm assurances that turbulence was normal. He sat in a window seat and watched in horror as the plane's wings seemed to flap. He waited for them to break off but miraculously the plane held together and eventually its undercarriage kissed the runway hello.

He was very happy to get his feet back onto something solid. Now he understood why people kissed the ground when they were finally liberated from a death trap like the one he was certain had been about to snuff out their young lives.

Once back in their familiar environment, the memories of their experiences in Hong Kong took on a surreal, dreamlike quality, as if they hadn't actually happened.

Ping would have given anything to wake up from what was easily the worst nightmare she'd ever had. How could they accuse her father of being a criminal? And not just a corporate criminal but a drug trafficker. The implications were almost as unbearable as they were unfair.

Fortunately none of their friends knew anything about what had happened and after being back in her routine for a few days, she was able to consign the entire incident into a slightly less immediately disturbing category. Ping was certain her father would be cleared of any wrong doing and within days had immersed herself back into student life.

Over the next term the news wasn't good. Her mother's condition deteriorated. Communication yielded nothing concerning her father's predicament. Silver linings remained elusive.

Tashi also immersed himself in his studies.

One of the great things about teeth is that almost everybody has some and they are an anomaly in an otherwise well designed, functionally efficient human body. Evolution had been particularly negligent in choosing them as the primary processing equipment for the vital function of eating.

In the current dietary reality, teeth are the source of extreme pain in anybody who neglects their welfare. Tashi found them fascinating. They were so vital to a person's health and yet most people preferred to ignore them until the consequences became unbearable. The modern western style diet had invaded China as convincingly as any other imperial phenomenon in history.

McDonalds and KFC stores competed with Starbucks and Dunkin Donuts to wreak havoc in the mouths of people who thought that being seen frequenting these purveyors of salt, sugar and fat was fashionable, a sign of sophistication and status. They were the worst thing that could ever have happened to the concept of dental health. Neither of his parents had ever suffered from tooth decay, but dentistry was an industry that was growing more rapidly than any other sector in an economy that was doubling every five years.

Pollution, greed and rotten teeth were the inevitable consequences of modern living. They were the price that had to be paid so China could become the super-power it rightfully always had been and he intended to be part of the solution to the problem. He had chosen a profession that granted quality of life to people who would otherwise suffer horribly. Dentistry was compassionate and essential.

Ping disagreed. She thought teeth were like plumbing, a necessary evil that should be left to somebody else. Studying teeth steadfastly failed to qualify as an intellectual pursuit on her list of academic imperatives. She tried to convince Tashi that he should become a lawyer or a doctor or anything that wasn't as practical and boring as a dentist.

But despite this they continued to enjoy every moment they could steal from the stifling jaws of academia. Their relationship flourished and, as the term approached its inevitable end, a plan to visit Tashi's family was reaching fruition in Ping's mind.

Tashi's mind was less enthusiastic. He wasn't ashamed of his family but he didn't think they would appreciate Ping or she them.

* * *

Ping and Tashi met every Tuesday afternoon in the park near the library, when they both had an hour of free time before their next lecture. When Ping arrived one afternoon fresh from an Archeology tutorial, she had a picture of an object that bore a remarkable resemblance to the one in her father's painting.

"It's the Oracle of Singh Ma," she announced proudly.

"No, it doesn't look anything like that," Tashi lied.

"Of course it does," affirmed Ping. "This is what's in my father's painting. I recognised it immediately."

"The thing I found has pictures etched into it."

"Even better. The Oracle of Singh Ma is a legendary symbol. It predates the Bon religion."

"What's the Bon religion?" asked Tashi.

"It was the dominant Tibetan religion before Buddhism arrived."

"I thought Buddhism originated in Tibet," said Tashi, slightly affronted by the suggestion that the pre-eminent cultural icon of his homeland hadn't originated there.

"Buddhism came from India," Ping informed him. "It was introduced into Tibet by Padma Sambhava, a Buddhist saint in the seventh or eighth century."

"Are you sure?" Tashi asked in disbelief.

"Of course I'm sure. The Buddha was an Indian Prince. He was born in modern day Nepal. He wasn't Tibetan."

"Yes he was," said Tashi stubbornly.

"What, so you're a Buddhist now?"

"No. I don't believe in ancient superstition."

"I'm pleased to hear that," countered Ping.

"So this oracle thing is really ancient?" asked Tashi attempting to steer the conversation away from his freshly exposed cultural ignorance.

"It's at least 5,000 years old. Probably even older."

"Give me another look," he said.

Ping flicked through the pages of her book and arrived back at the picture.

"Yes, that's it," confirmed Tashi. "But I've only got half of it."

"Where's the other half?"

"I don't know. I took one half and my friend Wen took the other. I haven't seen him since I was about twelve. His family had lots of problems and they moved away from our village."

"Well if you've got half of the Oracle of Singh Ma, it will still be a very significant discovery."

"It's probably not the original."

"What's it made of?"

"It's some kind of really hard crystal. I don't know. I'd never seen anything like it. Is it supposed to have any kind of practical function?"

"According to this book, the Oracle first appeared in a vision some monk had during his meditation."

"A vision?"

"The book says that a Buddhist monk in the 12th Century, during his meditation, had a vision. In his vision he saw the end of the world and then he saw the Oracle of Singh Ma and the earth was healed."

"You're joking!"

"No. It says here that the Oracle represents a healing energy that will flood from the cosmos and stop the apocalypse as it is happening."

"What? It's going to save us from the apocalypse? Do they say which particular apocalypse it's going to save us from?"

"I don't know. I just read this stuff."

"Great! You keep reading that stuff and I'll keep learning how to fix people's teeth."

"Don't be so cynical. If you've found a physical manifestation of this thing, it's an esoteric icon. It's not of this world."

"What world is it of then? If I found it, it can't be from any worlds that are that far away. Is it going to bring us good luck?"

Ping rolled her eyes.

"Sorry," said Tashi. "I'm a practical guy. All this esoteric stuff doesn't mean much to me. You're the space cadet. What does it mean? Is it valuable?"

"How dare you call me a space cadet?"

And with that Ping got up and stormed away with her book firmly wedged under an uncompromising arm.

Shocked, Tashi followed her. He knew she'd won. If she really had found a picture of the thing he and Wen had found, there was no way he was going to prevent her from visiting his family. She had the ultimate excuse.

"I'm sorry, I wasn't serious."

Ping turned and began to cry.

"What's the matter?"

"It's my father," said Ping. "The case against him isn't going well. My mother thinks he's going to stay in jail for a long time."

"Surely they'll clear him. He's not a criminal."

"I hope so. My mother is losing hope."

"Don't worry, my darling. Things will work out. You'll see."

* * *

The train journey felt as though it was never going to end. Tashi hated it because he imagined that Ping must also be hating it. The worst part was that she never complained once. She even pretended to be enjoying it.

Tashi had always travelled third class, hard seat. He'd never thought to do otherwise.

Ping, however, wanted to fly to Lhasa and travel first class back to Nagqu. There was absolutely no circumstance under which Tashi was prepared to allow her to pay his fare back to Tibet. Even though the money meant nothing to her, it was the last bastion, the line in the sand that his pride would not cross. That meant the train, all 28 hours of it. If he stretched his budget to its absolute limit he could almost afford to pay what he considered an exorbitant fare and travel second class, hard sleeper but Ping still had to pay for herself.

The small compartment contained six bunks stacked three on each side, so they had to share with another four passengers. There was no door separating them from the narrow corridor and the only seating available was in the corridor outside the compartment unless they wanted to lie on their bunks. Ping happily engaged two of the other passengers in conversation and was very pleased to discover that they came from a village not far from Tashi's. Ping thought this meant they had something in common. Tashi didn't want to have anything in common with ordinary Tibetans. He dreaded the moment Ping realised what she was really dealing with. He knew he was heading irreversibly towards her realisation of just how humble it was possible for a human being's origins to be.

Tashi didn't sleep very well that night, despite being on a second tier bunk that was actually quite comfortable compared to previous journeys he'd spent trying to sleep on the hard seats. Ping was on the bunk next to his with one of the passengers she'd befriended snoring loudly on the bunk above her. Tashi could tell by the way she kept tossing and turning, she wasn't sleeping very well either.

The sound of the train was barely able to compete with an array of sleep related noises being randomly emitted throughout the carriage.

As the sun rose Tashi was unable to suppress the joy he felt at the sight of the prayer flags that began to appear scattered across the barren countryside as they gained altitude, speeding towards the Tibetan plateau. Their bright colours and random placement contrasted with the uniform silver power pylons that marched purposefully beside the railway track, symbols of progress, order and power.

Similarly, the closer they got to Tibet, the orderly, clean white sheep were gradually being infiltrated by yaks. Yaks are not orderly, clean or white. They are large, dirty, multi-coloured beasts that lumber around the countryside like lost, drunken hooligans. Tashi felt like a yak pretending to be a sheep.

By the time Ping finally gave up on her battle with semi-unconsciousness, Tashi was suffering from chest pains. He'd internalised his discomfort, having barely eaten on the journey and was dehydrated.

Ping rolled over and greeted him with a fresh Chinese smile that made him feel even dirtier than a yak. He felt like dried yak dung. If only somebody would set him on fire, so he could escape and float away on the cool mountain breeze.

Finally, halfway through the morning, the dreaded moment arrived. The squeal of the train's un-oiled brake drums, accompanied by a lurching decrease in velocity, signified that unavoidable, ultimate humiliation was upon him.

Ping tactfully refrained from pointing out that they'd stopped at a railway station which was the only man-made structure in sight.

Several yaks stared at the train as if it was the first they'd ever seen.

Tashi's mother and father were waiting on the platform. His mother had worn her best dress and his father looked like he was going to a temple. They'd managed to find clothes that insisted they were poor peasants. He could see them smiling expectantly amongst the few others meeting the train as it pulled up at the platform. Ping looked more like a Chinese princess than ever.

Tashi resisted a sudden urge to pretend they hadn't arrived yet and stay on the train. His mother's expectant smile was too strong a beacon for him to ignore.

The small part of him that wasn't utterly ashamed of his humble origins was proud that both his parents had obviously devoted time and effort to their appearance and had come to meet them.

The very idea that he'd fallen in love with a Chinese girl constituted heresy to some of the less tolerant members of the small village he had been so desperate to leave behind forever. The colloquial expression, 'the toad wants to eat the swan's meat,' referred to Tibetans (toads) who married into rich, Chinese (swans) families. It was a less than flattering description of his predicament. He had no way of knowing how his parents were going to react to Ping and was certain that a lot of his old neighbours would be openly hostile.

The pain had dropped to his stomach. Almost unbearably he helped Ping drag their bags down from the overhead storage rack. They clambered unsteadily towards the exit and down onto the platform.

Tashi's reticence was instantly swallowed up by the radiance of his mother's smile, which she quickly adapted to smothering him with kisses.

Ping stood back while his father fidgeted uncertainly. At the extreme periphery of his vision, Tashi could see the awkwardness looming between them. His father maintained his distance until Tashi was able to disentangle himself from his mother and affect a formal introduction.

Tashi's mother threw herself at Ping like an out of control hugging machine. Ping appeared to be delighted and allowed herself to be hugged and kissed before a more formal acceptance of Tashi's father's hand, which she enthusiastically shook.

It all seemed to be going quite well until his father, who insisted on carrying both their bags, unexpectedly led them to an area which was the local equivalent of a car park. There were no cars. The slowly subsiding pain in Tashi's stomach suddenly exploded into an entire new wave of agony.

"The co-op let us bring the new tractor," explained Tashi's mother proudly as his smiling father loaded their bags onto its trailer. Ping politely declined his father's offer to ride up front with him on the tractor itself and his mother helped them both climb aboard the trailer.

The trailer shook as the new diesel engine spluttered to life, sending a cloud of black acrid smoke up into the otherwise pristine, cloudless blue sky.

Ping's Tibetan was very limited. She'd been studying it for less than two years and had never before had an opportunity to speak to any actual Tibetans besides Tashi, who preferred to speak Mandarin. She attempted to engage Tashi's mother in conversation, pausing occasionally to blast him with a bright smile until Tashi's aching guts felt like they were going to explode.

Falsehood!

Where was it? Something was horribly false. It wasn't his parents. They weren't sophisticated enough to be false. It wasn't Ping. She seemed to be genuinely interested in trying to engage his mother and was working diligently to understand his mother's attempts to tell her about his childhood and youth.

That only left him, Tashi. He was the false link in the puzzle. He was the pretentious fraud. Suddenly it hit him. He didn't have to feel personally responsible for spanning the mammoth void he'd imagined would loom between Ping and his family. Besides the obvious language barrier, they were all getting along wonderfully.

The road wasn't much more than a rough track as they bumped and rattled through the semi-deserted countryside.

The pain in his stomach began to subside once again. The sound of his mother's and Ping's laughter mixed together, every time they bounced over a particularly deep pothole, soothingly infused itself into the tortured knot in his mid-rift.

From a distance, the village of Womadige was barely a speck on the flanks of Mt Luguna.

The pain returned instantly as he spotted his childhood home. The memory of Ping's father's mansion almost caused him to vomit.

"What's the matter?" asked Ping innocently as Tashi's smiling father pushed forward the throttle lever and brought the tractor to a halt.

Tashi felt like a fish on a hook. All he could do was struggle and the more he struggled the worse things got.

"Nothing," he muttered feebly, helping his father lift his old bag and Ping's designer label luggage from the trailer.

As he approached the shameful shack of his youth, a familiar sight cut through his inner pain, awakening memories.

"Free Chow!" he exclaimed as an overweight black and white cat came running out onto the track to meet them.

Tashi dropped the bag he'd refused to allow his father to carry and fell onto one knee as the purring feline approached.

"It's my cat!" he explained redundantly, picking up the old tom.

The rest of the conversation was lost in the sound of rapturous purring.

Inside his parents' house, little had changed. The old familiar sights and some of his discarded feelings flooded back. There was the smell of yak butter tea and yak dung smoke.

Where Ping had grown up on marble floors and antique rugs, as a child he'd played on these same hard packed earth floors. He looked into her eyes, trying to detect an element of distaste or condescension. He saw none.

He showed Ping the bedroom she would be sleeping in for the duration of their visit.

"Sorry we don't have a marble staircase."

"I've always hated marble."

"Me too."

Ping produced an exquisitely wrapped package from her suitcase.

"This is for your parents," she explained.

"What is it?"

"A surprise," she answered.

Tashi's parents were preparing food. Yak butter tea was boiling on the stove as Tashi followed Ping into the kitchen.

"This is for you," said Ping handing the exquisite gift to Tashi's mother.

Tashi's mother flashed her husband a look of utter confusion before wiping her hands on her apron and accepting the gift.

"Thank you," she said managing a weak smile. "I'll put it near the spirit house."

"You have to unwrap it," Ping said in Tibetan, mispronouncing most of the words.

Tashi's mother fired another even more confused look at her husband.

Tashi translated Ping's instruction into something his mother could grasp.

"Here, let me help you," offered Tashi.

"No, let your mother unwrap it," insisted Ping.

Tashi's father came to his wife's assistance but was unable to offer any practical help.

Ping retrieved the gift and demonstrated how to remove the outer layer of paper before handing it back to Tashi's mother. She took it and hesitantly continued the process to reveal a box containing four small replicas of terra cotta warriors from Xi'an. Tashi's mother handed the gift to her husband, who smiled and nodded in polite confusion.

"They're terra cotta warriors from Xi'an," Ping tried to explain.

"They are for decoration," added Tashi, attempting to drag two parallel universes into the same dimension.

"Ah," said his father unhelpfully.

FOUR - UNIFICATION

The next morning Tashi woke up early. The pain he experienced when he awoke was less than excruciating for the first time in 48 hours and continued to diminish as he got out of bed and dressed himself.

Out in the kitchen his mother had the fire roaring and was ready with hot yak butter tea.

Ping emerged from her bedroom a few minutes later and bid everyone a happy afternoon. She looked slightly confused as they all laughed. Tashi pointed out her mistake and she re-issued her greeting, swapping morning for afternoon. Both Tashi's parents smiled in appreciation of her attempts to communicate in a language which up until their arrival had been little more than a collection of academic noises. The pain in Tashi's stomach continued to become more bearable over breakfast but lingered threateningly for the rest of the morning.

Lunch had it on the run. The fresh organic food he hadn't experienced since leaving home marched triumphantly through his grateful gut, restoring his sense of health and wellbeing. Ping appeared to have been accepted by his parents and the terra cotta warriors were occupying a place of honor on the large wooden cabinet which dominated the living area. By late afternoon the pain had been thoroughly vanquished and that evening he ate as if he had a vacuum cleaner for a stomach.

The trunk in the attic remained undisturbed for another day while Tashi took Ping on a tour of some of the magical places which had enchanted his childhood. The other villagers maintained a respectful distance, returning Tashi's greetings and some even returning Ping's smile.

The next morning, at Ping's insistence, the trunk was manhandled down from the attic, landing roughly on the hard dirt floor.

"I think it's in here," said Tashi.

A selection of his childhood chattels were ripped unceremoniously from their sanctuary, exposing the tip of an object wrapped in green cloth.

"I was sure I wrapped it in blue cloth," said Tashi affecting a non-dental extraction.

"It's beautiful," said Ping as the object was unwrapped.

"It's a lot smaller than I remember," said Tashi.

"I wonder what these symbols mean," said Ping ignoring his disappointment and lovingly taking hold of the object. "It feels warm."

"So would you if you'd been stuck up in that attic with all that other junk."

"We need to find the other half," declared Ping.

"That's not going to be easy. I haven't seen Wen for years."

"Somebody must know where he is."

"He may not have it any more."

"Something like this couldn't just disappear. Anybody can see that it's beautifully made and totally unique."

"We're farmers. It's not useful."

"If this really is half of the Oracle of Singh Ma, it's incredibly valuable. And even if it isn't the genuine article, it must be very old."

"What do you want with that old thing?" asked Tashi's mother from the kitchen.

"Do you or dad know what happened to Wen?" asked Tashi, ignoring her question.

"Wen's family moved to a village south of here. I heard he died in a fire about two years ago."

"He died?" It had been a long time but special childhood friends never entirely leave your heart. Tashi sat down as a wave of grief crashed over him.

"What's the matter?" asked Ping, whose knowledge of Tibetan hadn't covered the subject of death.

"My friend Wen is dead," Tashi translated.

"That doesn't mean we can't still find the other half," insisted Ping, ignoring Tashi's sudden sadness. "Where did he die? Somebody must know where it is."

"Do you know which village?" asked Tashi attempting to recover from his sudden sullen slump.

"I think they went to Daru," said Tashi's mother.

"How far away is it?" asked Ping, recognising Daru as a location.

"Not far. It's on the other side of Mt Luguna," said Tashi.

"When can we go?"

"What? My mother just said he's dead."

"That doesn't mean the Oracle is gone. It must still be somewhere. Don't you realize, you may have found something ancient, rare and extremely valuable?"

* * *

Two days later they were on the road. Tashi borrowed his father's cart and attempted to reacquaint himself with its workings. He'd never liked horses and this particular one had thrown him when he tried to ride it a few years earlier. Fortunately it didn't remember him.

Ping had never ridden on a cart before. Her first experience of family transportation that didn't involve a chauffeur and plush leather seats had been riding on the tractor trailer when they arrived. The horse amazed her as it navigated the treachery of the mountain track.

The air tasted intangibly sweet and she could feel the snow in her bones. The chill in the air energised her imagination as they passed a sparse assortment of small dwellings, stimulating her wonder at the ancient methods Tibetans still employed to survive in such a harsh environment.

Then she began to wonder at the birds and insects. They lacked the rudimentary shelter the people had built and yet somehow seemed to be thriving. It was summer and the snows had ascended to the peaks of distant mountains but the thought of what existence must be like during the freezing winter months made her shiver.

Beyond was a valley and the imposing bulk of Mt Luguna.

The journey lasted almost the whole morning. As the sun reached its zenith they arrived at the village where Wen's family had reportedly moved.

Tashi asked a farmer they passed, if he knew anything about Wen or his family. The man had lived in the village all his life and directed them to the site where Jim's house had once stood. As they approached the place where his closest childhood friend had died, sadness filled his heart once again.

He pulled on the reigns and attempted to guide the obstinate horse to pull over. The horse did it's best to ignore him. Eventually human intelligence prevailed over whatever happens inside a horse's head and the cart belatedly drew to a halt, further down the track than intended.

The charred remnants of the house stood in stark contrast with the rest of the well-maintained village.

Situated on a small mound of barren brown earth, away from the inhabited dwellings, the mud brick walls were slowly being reclaimed. Despite the interceding two years, the aroma of burnt wood hung over the ruins like a badly written invitation to stay away.

Inside the crumbling walls, a few scorched, empty whiskey bottles were the only reminder that the place had once been a human dwelling. Tashi began poking randomly beneath the dirt with a charred stick. Ping was more purposeful and managed to find some old rusting springs that had once been part of a mattress.

"This looks like it was probably the bedroom," she said. Tashi followed her and forlornly applied his stick to the morbid task of excavation. It didn't take long to dig out a large section from where the bed had once stood. Ping found an old syringe and pieces of a broken vase. Tashi dug up a door handle as Ping produced some other handles that had probably been part of a dressing table.

They continued in silence for another twenty minutes, unearthing more sorry relics.

"Here it is!" announced Tashi, pulling what looked like a vaguely triangular lump of rock out of the dirt.

Ping took it from him and began to rub the charred earth from around it. The black crystal shone in the afternoon light.

"That's it!" she confirmed, flashing him a smile.

Although it had been two long winters since the house had burnt down, Tashi imagined he could still smell burning flesh. Obsessed by what she was holding, Ping didn't seem to even recognise the emotions he was suffering, or care about the sad fate of his childhood companion.

"It doesn't appear to have been damaged," she exclaimed as they exited the charred wreckage and walked triumphantly towards the horse which was attempting to make a meal out of some lonely shrubs beside the track.

* * *

By the time they arrived back in Womadige, the dirty triangular lump had been polished and restored to the closest state to its former glory it had exhibited for several sooty years. The sun was casting its last superfluous rays between the mountains as cold shadows devoured his childhood home.

"We found the other half of the Oracle," announced Ping proudly as they entered the warm kitchen.

"What?" asked Tashi's mother.

"Ungh?" inquired Tashi's father.

"We found the other half of that ornament, the one Wen and I found on Mt Luguna," explained Tashi.

This failed to elicit any further curiosity and no more questions were asked about the black object Ping was proudly displaying.

"Did you see Wen's mother?" asked Tashi's mother.

"No," replied Tashi. "But we found the house where he died. It was very sad."

"Where did you put your half?" asked Ping.

* * *

The pain in Tashi's stomach only returned briefly the next afternoon when a small group of villagers assembled outside his parent's house, hoping to catch a glimpse of the beautiful, Chinese girl they'd heard he'd brought home. They loitered for an hour but dispersed when Tashi's mother opened the front door and invited them inside for a cup of tea.

The next day it was time to catch the train back to Xi'an.

The trip had been a complete success.

As they were preparing to leave for Nagqu railway station, Tashi's mother gave Ping a present. It was a very old pair of turquoise and Himalayan coral earrings. They had been given to her by her mother-in-law when she and Tashi's father were married. They were a family heirloom whose origins receded back through many generations of the women in Tashi's family.

Tashi was both pleased and mortified.

He was very happy his mother had given the earrings to Ping because it meant his parents accepted Ping into the family. Most ethnic Tibetans opposed their children marrying Chinese, believing the Chinese had done immeasurable damage to Tibetan culture by destroying monasteries and murdering monks since the invasion of Tibet in 1958.

They had exiled the Dalai Lama, the spiritual and political leader of the Tibetan people and flooded Tibet with 25 million Han Chinese, who now outnumbered the Tibetans by five to one. Tibetans were second class citizens in their own country. They were forbidden to practice their unique form of Buddhism and were constantly harassed by soldiers and the police, controlled by the government in distant Beijing.

The capital city of Lhasa had suffered unspeakable atrocities as cultural imperialism insisted that one of the most spiritually advanced societies on Earth renounce their cherished beliefs and conform to the dictates of the spiritually inert elite in Beijing.

The earrings were a powerful symbol, but Tashi was afraid a wealthy Chinese woman would find them ugly and primitive, the stones unpolished and the silver dull. He couldn't imagine Ping ever wearing them. He had seen the contents of her jewelry box, laden with precious stones and golden trinkets.

However, despite his misgivings, Ping appeared ecstatic. She understood that the gift symbolised her acceptance by Tashi's family. That was worth far more than money.

She also knew the value of genuine turquoise which is rare. The vast majority of turquoise available in markets and shops was in fact hard plastic, sold to the gullible and ignorant who had never seen the real thing.

She hugged and kissed Tashi's mother while Tashi and his father stood back and enjoyed the generational moment.

Then the four of them squashed themselves, and Ping's and Tashi's luggage onto the cart to make the journey to Nagqu railway station. The tractor was being used to drag boulders from the river so it wasn't available for the return journey. The horse whinnied a brief protest at the extra weight before resigning itself to the task.

Tashi and Ping waved a teary goodbye from the train windows as Tashi's parents and Nagqu railway station slowly receded from view.

Despite the complete absence of any luxury, the trip had ended far more successfully than Tashi's first visit to Hong Kong. Not only had nobody been arrested or hospitalized, they had the Oracle of Singh Ma, or a very convincing copy, packed safely inside Ping's luggage. They sat contentedly together on a bottom bunk as the rugged countryside flashed past.

Tashi suspected it was the same train. He spent most of the first afternoon trying to locate familiar aspects of the carriages that would confirm his belief.

By the time it was dark he'd given up. Trains all looked the same. They sounded the same and smelt the same. They were the same even when they were different.

The return journey back to Xi'an was far less painful. The dread and fear that had grown progressively more oppressive going the other way had all proved unfounded.

They were young. They had each other and time on their side. The mountains were replaced by the dry monotony of the Gobi Desert, which eventually surrendered to more interesting vistas of trees, hills and rivers.

Suddenly, or so it seemed, lost as they had been in each other's company, they were back in Xi'an.

The traffic was still fighting to arrive before itself, the sky was hidden behind an enormous canopy of stale pollution and the air was warm and humid. Nothing appeared to have changed since they left, a stark contrast to the myriad inner transformations they had experienced.

They boarded another train and within half an hour were back in Xian'yang.

Nobody was waiting to meet them and the university didn't appear particularly interested in where they had been or what they had done.

That was until the afternoon of Ping's first archaeology tutorial.

"What's that supposed to be?" asked Professor Guo.

"It's either the Oracle of Singh Ma itself or a very old copy," claimed Ping proudly.

"The Oracle of Singh Ma was blue," said the professor dismissively. "Give it to me," he added with professorial disinterest etched into every learned syllable.

"Where did you get this?" he asked.

"Mt Luguna."

"Where's that?"

"Tibet."

"Ungh?"

The silence that followed smelled strongly of traffic and stale duck.

"Can I take this away for examination?"

"No. The wind is strong and I need it as a paper weight," teased Ping.

The learned professor looked beyond his glasses for the first time in several semesters. He was young in professorial terms, being in his mid thirties, tall, thin, unmarried and lacking a developed sense of humor. He sported a Spartan growth on his upper lip which looked like somebody had attempted to sew his lips together with a few strands of wispy black cotton but had somehow missed his mouth. He'd spent all of his short existence engrossed in academic study and appeared awkward in the presence of attractive female students.

"Of course," corrected Ping as the trafficky, ducky silence threatened to merge with the sweet smell of her own perfume.

This was followed by an even more meaningful, "Ungh."

Later that afternoon, when Ping returned to her flat after lectures were concluded, she was surprised to find Professor Guo waiting on her doorstep.

"Can I come in?" he asked after a brief exchange of courtesies.

"Of course."

Once inside, he produced the Oracle from his bag.

"Where exactly did you get this?" he asked, this time displaying genuine interest.

"My friend, Tashi found it on Mt Luguna in Tibet when he was a boy."

"This could be the greatest find since the terracotta warriors," he declared, throwing traditional discretion to the wind. "I've already checked with the major museums. It's too early to know for sure, but nobody seems to know of anything quite like it. A colleague of mine, who specialises in rare antiquities, is on his way from Beijing to examine it personally. He should be here tomorrow morning. Have you told anybody else about this?"

"Besides Tashi who told me about it, no I haven't."

"Good! Until we can verify its authenticity, I think we should keep it to ourselves."

"Is it valuable?'

"I can't be sure at this stage. Do you mind if I keep it in the faculty safe until it can be properly examined?"

"Not at all."

FIVE - IRFAN MULLARAMZAN

In a remote village in the mountains of central Tibet, an ancient spiritual rite was nearing conclusion. The monks from Sera Monastery had located the reincarnation of one of Tibet's greatest spiritual masters. The seven-year-old boy had correctly selected the old master's rosary beads, his cloak and finally his bowl, from amongst four similar objects. He had addressed one of the more elderly in the official party by his first name and recognised him as his old retainer.

Outside, across the valley spread a magnificent rainbow.

The boy had been waiting a long time for somebody to come and find him and as far as he was concerned they were late. He'd formed many attachments in the village and now he knew they would soon be gone forever. His purpose and his destiny had finally arrived.

The news of the discovery of the young tulku and his confirmation spread up the valley's and away to Lhasa and beyond. The sacred syllables 'om mani padme hum' danced playfully in the clear mountain air. Giant trumpets blasted out guttural bass notes which echoed around the mountains to the accompaniment of hand symbols and yak bells.

After the initial celebrations were concluded, it was getting late and the senior monks wanted to begin the long journey back to their Monastery with their prized discovery.

Meanwhile, not far away, a man was having his throat cut in a well-lit cave. The executioner was rough and even though the blade was sharp, it was a messy spectacle that Irfan did not want to witness.

He had known all the three traitors personally. When he first heard they were the betrayers, Irfan was sure it must be a mistake. But then the evidence began to mount until even he was overwhelmed beyond reasonable doubt.

Watching Omar die tore at his heart strings. The others had died trying to escape once they'd been found. Omar was asleep in bed with his wife when his executioners arrived before dawn. Besides losing a few teeth and suffering two black eyes, he was captured easily.

At the final moment Irfan looked away.

He'd never expected to be witnessing an execution. Until three weeks earlier he'd been a humble drug courier. His job had been to lead a pack of mules along the ridge then down to the river several villages beyond the mountains in the direction of the rising sun. Once he got to the river he unloaded the cargo and gave it to Omar. He got paid when he returned with the mules. Irfan had been doing this now for nearly five years and had never witnessed any violence. He didn't have a gun or any weapons other than his knife, which had never been used on anything more dangerous than a tangled bridle.

Now it suddenly looked like he needed to find a new vocation very quickly, ideally working for a company that specialized in helicopter rescues for its new recruits. The cave behind him was packed with heroin. It had been building up since operations came to an abrupt halt almost a month before.

But that wasn't the worst aspect of the disasters unfolding around him. The gentle mountain breezes were whispering that they were all wanted men. Rumours abounded, like diseases in a dirty hospital. Irfan was worried that whatever he'd caught might keep him from ever seeing his wife and family in Kashmir again.

He had no idea how old he was. His mother had died when he was too young to remember and his father was a soldier fighting another war somewhere else. It was even possible that Irfan might be about to find himself fighting against his own father, if the rumors were correct and the military had been alerted and was moving against them.

A sudden, large explosion backed up that theory. The cave shook and dust filled the illuminated air. Irfan could smell fear. A lot of it was his own.

He had only wanted to make some money. He didn't use heroin himself but if other people wanted it, why shouldn't he get rich helping them get it? As far as he was concerned, he wasn't doing anything wrong.

He believed in Allah. And if it was Allah's will, he was happy to be sending poison to destroy the enemies of Islam. Allah had provided him with an opportunity to work as a holy warrior, and look after his family at the same time.

There was another explosion close to the mouth of the cave. The blast wave knocked him and everyone else off their feet. At that point self-preservation over rode any other impulse. Everyone panicked. Irfan got to his feet and ran to the cave mouth, fearing he would be buried alive.

Outside, the chill of early evening was waiting. His decision to run to the left was vindicated by an enormous explosion which destroyed everything more than ten metres away to his right.

Irfan was blown forward. He somersaulted twice and rolled up onto his feet. He didn't look back.

Merciful Allah had granted him another chance.

As he sprinted downhill, another explosion slammed into the cave behind him. A few small rocks caught his back, but otherwise he was uninjured.

Behind him the sounds of men screaming and general destruction grew more distant as he ran. He was on a downward slope and there were few obstacles.

Suddenly the moon appeared from behind a mountain.

He could see.

That meant he could be seen. He stopped abruptly and backed up into the shadows.

In the stillness he heard a sound like distant jungle drums beating out a rhythm that morphed into a sound he'd only ever heard on television. Helicopters. Troops were coming.

He forgot about being seen in the moonlight and began running with a renewed sense of panic.

He ran for a long time. The sound of helicopters receded behind him, but he could hear gunshots. Once again, he was swallowed by the welcoming darkness as the frequency of gunshots diminished to less than what he would have expected at a birthday party or wedding. On and on, into the night he ran. He thanked Allah with all the breath he could spare.

Time was less important. Distance was the most important thing as he sprinted onwards in his own private marathon. He ran all night, pausing only occasionally to drink from a river that was running down the mountainside with him.

In the irrelevance of time, the darkness slowly loosened its grip on his surroundings until sunlight flooded down onto the landscape.

Still he ran. His aching legs threatened to mutiny beneath him. He ignored the threats. They were no match for the reality he had left behind.

The sun rose into a clear blue sky but he continued to run. Run and drink. He thanked Allah for the cold mountain water which his body warmed and returned to the earth as sweat. It was no longer a sprint. His legs accepted the compromise but replaced their threats with pain. Pain was good. It meant he was still alive.

Suddenly a structure. Shelter and rest.

Allah be praised!

It was definitely a human dwelling. There had to be somebody nearby. Hopefully somebody with food they didn't mind sharing.

It was a lot to expect, but Irfan had a lot of faith. He was faithful to the point that even if he starved to death, he would believe it happened because Allah loved him.

The front door was a large slab of shale. Irfan didn't knock. Had there been a doorbell, he wouldn't have rung it. Emergencies like the one his life had become precluded such gentile considerations.

The place was empty. It looked like it had been empty for a long time as Irfan searched for food. There was none.

Even so, he fell to his aching knees, intending to give thanks for being alive. But before he could enunciate his first grateful sentence, sleep replaced prayer and oblivion replaced gratitude.

* * *

Outside, the sun shone but inside, the only ruling principle was exhaustion masquerading as lovable kittens delivering Ramadan blessings to the squirrels in the park.

He was dreaming!

Some people, released from Earthly limitations, are blessed to never wake up. Irfan didn't join their ranks on that day.

Reluctantly he awoke. Instantly he regretted everything.

The house hadn't collapsed on top of him and nobody was blowing anything up or trying to kill him.

That was a relief, but his legs were reminding him they'd made threats and the threats had been ignored. The air was fresh and the light warmed his toes.

The so-called room he slept in was little more than a lean-to against the side of a hill. Irfan arose. He forced his legs to hold him upright. They needed to get him to some food.

Run! Run? Well maybe just try to walk fast. Food would come in time. The most important thing was distance but time was now the major secondary concern. In his starving brain he hoped more time would mean more food.

Outside the freshly re-abandoned lean-to, Irfan moved towards the sunrise. Birds were singing and a gentle breeze animated a carpet of dandelions and buttercups dancing peacefully at his feet. He reached down and scooped up a handful. The flowers looked a lot better than they tasted. The second mouthful was less shocking. Fortunately the river, still running, was nearby. A few scoops of its highly athletic contents washed most of the bitter taste from his mouth.

Lacking other options, he stumbled forward. The lengthening shadows attested to the fact it was already late afternoon. By nightfall he was many more kilometres away from the cave. He felt marginally safer. The air was no longer polluted by the smell of high explosives and his friend's burnt flesh.

Just after sunset, he encountered a village. It was dirty and dilapidated. The greatest danger its peaceful façade threatened, was either from typhoid or leprosy. It looked like a good place to rot. Most of it already had.

Irfan was past being hungry. His body had realised the futility of screaming for food and given up. His stomach had joined his legs in a state of silent shock.

After executing his nearest approximation of a nonchalant stroll into town, he stepped into a tea house. Four men sucking on a hookah regarded the latest arrival in their domain. Irfan avoided eye contact, not interested in finding out if relaxed also meant friendly. He didn't need friends, he needed food.

Once again, he silently thanked Allah, this time for the contents of his pocket. He had been paid and was cashed up. He ordered food and found himself a deserted table in one of the establishment's darker corners.

The food arrived! Praise be to Allah!!!

He continued to thank Allah for his good fortune, between gulps.

After food, Irfan needed sleep. The establishment's representative behind the counter agreed to furnish him with a bed for the night. He was escorted out the back and shown into a small room.

* * *

"My archaeology professor is doing cartwheels!" declared an excited young Chinese woman on a university campus far away. "He's claiming the greatest archaeological discovery of the 21st Century!"

"Is it the real Oracle of Singh Ma?" asked Tashi when he and Ping met outside the library as they did every Tuesday afternoon.

"We can't exactly claim that to be 100% true. However he says it's the oldest representation ever found and its origins have yet to be determined. It really could be the actual Oracle of Singh Ma!"

"But wasn't that just a dream some monk had?"

"Yes, originally. But then it was said to have manifested in one of the monasteries. One afternoon, all the monks were bored and threatening to boycott meditation unless something concrete happened. And it did."

"Is this supposed to be some kind of fairy tale or something?"

"No, it's a legend. It was recorded by the monks in several monasteries and it's still taken seriously by some of the more obscure sects of Buddhism."

"So when do I get it back?"

"It's not that simple. Professor Guo wants to talk with you tomorrow morning. I told him you'd be available. I hope that's OK."

"I've got lectures until 10 and then I've got a half hour break. What does he want to talk about?"

"He wants to know exactly where you found it and how long you've had it. He's very excited!"

* * *

Irfan awoke. His legs skipped threatening and ached. He'd run too far, too fast and the rest of his body was also complaining.

Outside a noisy procession, containing the young master who'd been confirmed as a tulku, was passing through the village.

There was a jug of water in the room on an ancient sideboard. Irfan splashed some onto his face and then slipped out into the teahouse. It was deserted as he made his way out onto the street.

He was able to attach himself to the tail end of the procession which easily absorbed him as if by osmosis. The procession wound its way out of the village and into the countryside.

After another day, getting further away from the cave, he found himself setting up tents then preparing vegetables, and finally serving up food. Eventually he also got fed. It was a wonderful arrangement as far as he was concerned.

That night he was allowed to curl up beside a smouldering fire and the next morning was included in a pre-dawn breakfast before continuing with the procession.

All things are impermanent and the monks eventually reached their destination after nine days of travelling.

Irfan needed to keep moving. He didn't accept the promise of a bed, up the winding path that led to the monastery. Instead he made his excuses and departed from the monks as the path forked, offering a clear choice which Irfan had already made.

It was the wrong choice, for everyone. The young tulku had been removed from the head of the procession two days before its eventual arrival. The senior monks noticed an influx of mysterious young men pretending to be monks and realised they were being infiltrated. They put the tulku's young retainer on the throne and carried him into the waiting arms of the

Chinese authorities who arrested him before his feet had touched the cobblestones.

The young master was disguised as one of the servants and smuggled into a kitchen. For the next eight weeks, he was kept in hiding and moved between the monastery's many hidden rooms as the Chinese authorities systematically beat and tortured their way towards him through a protective crowd of devoted, but otherwise helpless monks.

Irfan's choice was similarly ill fated. After another two days travelling alone, he was walking along a paved road when a police car pulled up beside him.

"Where are you going?' asked an unpleasant looking Chinese policeman.

Irfan didn't bother to answer. He jumped over a small ditch and began running. Behind him he heard the policeman ordering him to stop. That merely spurred him to run faster.

A shot rang out and he felt a stinging pain in his left leg, as he fell forward onto his face.

At last one of his legs had backed up the threats.

SIX - THE SHARK

Several thousand kilometres away in sunny Shanghai, Dan Ban Ho was lying low. He had always known that one day he'd get caught and had spent a lot of time and energy insuring his personal interests would be kept separate from the consequences of that day. He had been scrupulous in removing all traces of himself from the lives of his army of underlings and recent history had vindicated his foresight. However that didn't guarantee the protection would hold forever. It depended on how much energy the authorities were prepared to invest in dismantling his meticulously constructed façade. So far he was just outside the police net, but he couldn't shake the uncomfortable feeling that there were sharks lurking in his swimming pool.

Dan Ban Ho decided it was time to pack up his wife and son and go on an indefinite holiday to Canada or Australia or anywhere large and relatively uninhabited. Anywhere he could blend into the local fauna until the situation returned to a closer approximation of his highly unorthodox concept of normality.

Getting pulled off an aeroplane in front of your wife and child is an utterly humiliating experience. Fortunately that didn't happen. Ho and his family were stopped as they tried to check in their luggage. That's also a very humiliating experience.

He could hear the music from the movie Jaws pumping away at the back of his brain as they were marched into a white office with a desk in front of a large mirror on the wall.

His nine-year-old son imagined they were getting special treatment because they were special. His wife was less easy to convince. She wasn't happy and Ho worked hard to avoid having to look her directly in the eye.

An unimpressive official in a grey uniform appeared and sat down behind the desk. He shuffled his papers with an impersonal authority that Ho found most irritating.

"What's the problem?" asked Ho.

* * *

"Please, step into my office," said Professor Guo, ushering Tashi into a spacious room sporting a solitary dead plant wilting sadly above one of several grey filing cabinets. The room was filled with smoke. The source appeared to be a rotund gentleman wearing a shabby brown suit, seated behind a large untidily laden desk.

"Would you like a cup of tea?"

Tashi wasn't accustomed to being treated so civilly by anybody, especially members of the university's staff.

"No thank you," he answered.

"This is Professor Xu. He's here from Beijing."

"Hello."

The Oracle was sitting on the desk in front of Professor Xu. He was much older than Professor Guo but appeared to be just as excited.

Professor Xu was of Mongolian extraction, short and fat. His body and head looked like two cubes welded together with a permanent cigarette drooping from the smaller of the two square oddities. His students in Beijing referred to him as 'old Rubix'. This was an observation inspired by the shape of his head and its tendency to display an impressive range of colours caused by high blood pressure and an unhealthy life style.

Professor Xu was married and had a 37 year old daughter who had emigrated to the U.S., leaving her parents trapped in a loveless union. He removed his spectacles.

"This is a most interesting find," he began.

"What is it?" asked Tashi.

The much taller, much younger, Professor Guo looked to his colleague before answering. "We're not entirely sure. We haven't been able to decipher any of the symbols so we can't say definitively where it originated or from what period."

"What can you say about it?" asked Tashi.

"It appears to be very old," said Professor Xu, stubbing out a cigarette in an overflowing ashtray. "I've studied ancient artefacts for nearly 40 years and I must confess I've never seen anything like it."

"Is it the Oracle of Singh Ma?" asked Tashi.

"The Oracle of Singh Ma is a mythical object," replied the older professor. "Nobody has ever seen it, if in fact it does actually exist. We are currently searching for references to it in the literature that survived in Buddhist monasteries. This process will take some time because the monasteries don't have a central library and don't share their records. Most of the records were destroyed during the Cultural Revolution. We were hoping you could tell us exactly where the object was found."

"Near the summit of Mt Luguna."

"How did you find it?"

"I was climbing the mountain with a friend. We dislodged a plant and it fell out of the cliff."

"I have some maps. Could you pinpoint the exact location for us?"

"I'll try," said Tashi as Professor Guo placed a map of Tibet in front of him.

"It was here," he said pointing to the spot. "Just below the summit."

"Thank you," said Professor Xu replacing his spectacles and staring at the map as Professor Guo hovered behind him.

* * *

"They couldn't tell me anything," said Tashi when he met Ping in the cafeteria half an hour later.

"I don't think they know any more than we do," said Ping. "Did they give it back?" she asked.

"No. They said they needed to study it some more before they can determine exactly what it is and where it originally came from."

"I have to go back to Hong Kong," said Ping, abruptly changing the subject. "My father's trial is about to start and my mother needs my support."

"How's she coping?'

"Not very well. I spoke with her while you were in your meeting and she sounded terrible."

"When are you going?"

"My mother begged me to come back immediately. I told her I can't just leave my studies but I'll probably go next week."

"Any news about your father's trial?"

"He's got the best lawyers in Hong Kong working on his case. We don't know what evidence they have against him."

"If he's innocent they can't have very much."

"Of course he's innocent!"

"Did she have any idea how long the trial is likely to go on?"

"She's very heavily sedated. She's in a fantasy world. I think she's trying to pretend nothing has happened. Her sister, my aunty is looking after her but she wants me to come home."

"That's a shame. I need you to protect me from those crazy professors of yours. Did you meet Professor Xu?"

"No."

"He wouldn't last 10 minutes in the Dentistry Faculty. His eyes look in two different directions. He looks like something out of a horror movie."

"He's an expert on ancient artefacts"

"He acts more like an expert on ancient farty acts. He smelt really bad."

They both laughed.

* * *

Irfan awoke. He felt bad. His leg was worse than merely agonising. It screamed and stunk of pain. He was in a bed with starched white sheets and he tried to sit up but that proved to be a bad idea. His hands were tied.

The room began to come into focus. It was white and clean with a strong smell of disinfectant.

"Hello! Where am I?" he called.

An oversized police uniform containing a very skinny constable entered the room. Irfan's curiosity escaped.

"Good! You're awake," accused the undersized policeman in a language Irfan didn't understand.

"Where am I?" repeated Irfan hoping for an answer he could understand.

"Jail."

"What?"

"Just wait. Somebody is coming to talk to you."

Irfan spoke Kashmiri and Tibetan. Unaware he was doing as commanded, he waited.

* * *

Ping sat in the courtroom gallery. Her father smiled up at her as he sat with his hands cuffed in front of him in the dock. He looked smaller than she'd ever seen him, more like a solitary boulder than an entire quarry.

Dan Ban Ho was being cross examined. The chief prosecutor, Yu Dong was an unusually ugly man. The judge was even uglier. But neither of them could compete with the raw ugliness of Dan Ban Ho's testimony of depravity, greed and immorality. According to him, Ping's father was the leader of a well organised drug trafficking cartel which had been working out of Hong Kong for almost two decades.

"Can you identify the head of the cartel?" Yu Dong enquired smoothly.

"Yes," replied Ho.

"Is he in this courtroom?"

"Yes," replied Ho.

"Please point to him. The court stenographer can record that the witness is pointing at the accused sitting in the dock. Thank you Mr Dan. I have no further questions."

Sun Xuefa, the chief defense barrister, was an elegant man in his late fifties with a distinguished silver moustache beneath an impressive crop of silver hair. He rose slowly to his feet and glided towards the witness.

"Mr Dan, you are the CEO of an export business. Is that correct?"

"Yes."

"Is it therefore true to say that the defendant is one of your business competitors?"

"I'm not a drug smuggler, so no, we aren't competitors," replied Ho.

"But you and the defendant have engaged in competitive practices for export contracts in the past."

"Quite possibly."

"And is your business as successful as the defendant's business?"

"I wouldn't know. I've never seen his books."

"But surely you must have some idea."

"No."

"Thank you. That's all Mr Dan."

The judge appeared to have gone to sleep. One of the bailiffs approached the bench and administered a gentle judicial nudge. The judge grunted.

"Court is adjourned," he said.

"All rise," commanded the bailiff.

Ping stood respectfully as the judge went to find somewhere more comfortable to sleep and her father was led from the courtroom.

The next day Irfan was the star witness. Dan Ban Ho paid little attention to him as he was wheeled into the courtroom. For a few seconds Dan Ban Ho sat comfortably imagining that his meticulously concocted web of deceit was some form of security. At first he resisted the impulse of recognition. Then as it bludgeoned its way painfully into his reluctant awareness, he sat up and stared in disbelief at Irfan.

Irfan's eyes darted around the room like trapped birds searching for a perch. Eventually they found one.

Ho averted his eyes, desperately trying to control his facial geography. Suddenly betrayal was no longer his ally.

How had they found Irfan? Surely he'd been killed in the cave with the rest of them! How could he possibly have a dead man staring at him. A dead man waving a hangman's noose in his direction. He looked helplessly at his lawyer, who intuitively grasped the economic potential and smiled back.

Irfan would rather have been presenting his case at the gates of hell than here. At the gates of hell he would at least have his devotion to Allah to save him. Here he had nothing. Here he didn't even understand the language that was no doubt being used to prepare his execution; an execution that wouldn't even grant him the status of a martyr.

The court had provided an interpreter but the man was some book learned city geek with no understanding of the intricate subtleties of Kashmiri. He hadn't even heard of the specific dialect which was Irfan's mother tongue.

The courtroom was filled with the type of people Irfan had spent his entire life avoiding. These were the ones who had taken the man-made world of sin seriously. They had gratefully surrendered to the lies and foolishness, imagining they were serving their own interests without any understanding of what their interests really were. Besides being infidels, they were the mindless cogs that empowered the machinery of a godless state. And here they were demanding he create some form of reality for them in a world where reality was merely another option, where the victims were encouraged to imagine they were the victors. A world that was a recruiting ground for the denizens of hell.

Amongst the throng he had recognised one face, desperately trying to pretend it didn't recognise him. It was a face which had once ruled his world, a face which had once spat on everything that wasn't within its control. And now it was pretending it wasn't the face it had always been. Irfan attempted a smile.

"All rise. This court is now in session."

Irfan was prodded until he too rose to his feet, despite the pain in his slowly healing leg.

Into the court came a caricature. It was hunched, ugly and wearing a costume that would have gotten it stoned to death on the streets where Irfan grew up.

"Bang!" went a fake wooden gavel on a fake wooden bench.

Irfan was asked a series of mostly meaningless questions. The interpreter glared at Irfan every time he failed to either translate the question correctly or understand Irfan's answer. Irfan did his best to convey to the damned fool questioning him, some obvious facts pertaining to his personal identity. Then he was asked about the identity of the face that was trying so hard not to be the face it was. He was asked if he recognised it. He was asked about the circumstances that compelled him to recognise it. Irfan was even asked about why the face in question was so obviously trying not to recognise him.

Then another, more personable court official directed the translator to ask him some more questions. These questions were a lot easier to answer. These questions weren't attempting to make him feel stupid and were more concerned with the truth. He did his best to be truthful, even though he suspected he was signing his own death warrant.

He watched the face twitch and contort as he gave straight forward answers to the barrage of badly translated questions. At one point, the face looked squarely at him and appeared to be muttering curses. Then it stared at the ceiling before it was immersed in its hands as if it needed to be manually kept up off the floor.

At the end of the questions, Sun Xuefa thanked him for his testimony and an attendant wheeled him out of the courtroom.

Clearly audible glee erupted from the gallery. Ping couldn't help herself. After the seemingly irrefutable testimony of Dan Ban Ho, she'd almost resigned herself to the unpalatable conclusion that her father was a drug smuggler. At last there was hope.

Ping ran from the court room and fumbled excitedly with her cell phone. She needed to tell Tashi the wonderful news.

There was no point wasting good news on her mother, who had shut the entire situation out of her mind with tranquilisers. She'd been barricaded inside an imaginary fortress where her most complicated thoughts fluttered by like butterflies in a fairy garden.

Fortunately Tashi was in his dormitory and after a few minutes was directed to the communal telephone.

"Hello Tashi?"

"Hello Ping."

Their connection almost qualified as poetry, but they refrained from any indulgence in iambic pentameter or haiku as both attempted to cheer the other with good news. Ping had the upper hand as she was paying for the call and being a lady went first.

"They have a witness who knows the cartel's leader personally. He's been able to positively identify my father's main accuser. He was shot in the leg when they arrested him in the mountains and needed an interpreter, but his testimony was very strong. I believed every word he said."

"That's wonderful."

"Yes. He said he'd met the cartel's leader on several occasions. He confessed to being one of the drug couriers who brought the drugs from the Pakistani border, through Kashmir and into Tibet. I'm so happy!"

"I also have some very good news," countered Tashi.

"What about?"

"The Oracle of Singh Ma."

"Have they found out whether it's authentic?"

"Almost. Professor Guo thinks he's deciphered some of the symbols on it. He copied them and fed them into a computer."

"Wow! What do they mean?"

"He's not completely sure yet but he thinks they're instructions which when fully understood, will allow us to unlock some kind of message contained inside it."

"That's pretty amazing."

"He said it's some kind of time capsule."

"When does he expect to be able to unlock its message?"

"The computer is still analysing the symbols. There are several probable meanings but he's not exactly sure which is the correct interpretation."

"That's awesome! A time capsule from the past. Does he know how old it is?"

"Not yet. He thinks that once he's unlocked its message, all will be revealed. So when are you coming back?"

"I don't know. The prosecutor is cross examining the new witness tomorrow. They'll be trying to undermine his testimony and find flaws in it. It depends how successful they are."

"Well at least somebody's backing up your father."

"I know. Isn't it fantastic? After hearing the last few days of evidence, I'd all but given up."

"Don't worry, my darling. I told you everything will work itself out properly in the end."

The rest of the conversation degenerated into Tashi's description of a new type of noodle being served in the cafeteria. It was a gallant effort to avoid the last real topic, which was how much they missed each other. The magnificent edifice they'd spent months creating atop the solid foundation of their unspoken lust, swayed in the gentle breeze of their shared longing.

SEVEN - FAILURE

Tashi continued to attend lectures and tutorials as if nothing unusual was happening. He earnestly applied himself to the study of teeth. Mostly he learnt about unhealthy teeth that were rotten, diseased and non-functional. He also learnt about gums, germs and general anatomy. His life was a veritable dental swamp where he sloshed around in puddles so deep, even the mud curdled into a conspiracy of rival germ colonies facing each other across a dark expanse of warm, moist tongue.

Ping stayed in Hong Kong where she slept on the couch in Aixia's small apartment. She'd missed her old friend. She hadn't managed to make any real new friends in Xian'yang. Most of her classmates were studying to become guides at the museum that housed Xi'an's famous terra cotta warriors. They'd been brought up under the communist system and knew very little about anything else. They were friendly enough but she found them shallow and very ignorant of anything to do with the world outside mainland China. She blamed the one child policy for producing a generation of spoilt brats with no real ambition to do anything other than conform to the Communist Party's dictates, get married young and have a spoilt conformist child, just like them. The boys were even worse, outnumbering the girls and devoting most of their spare time to leering at them from an uncomfortable distance.

That was one of the reasons why she'd been attracted to Tashi. He was an outsider like her and though he professed to admire the Chinese, he had experienced and seen far more than most of his classmates, despite his humble origins. Besides that, he was exotic, handsome and very strong, qualities she and Aixia discussed well into the night over a variety of alcoholic stimulants.

Aixia had several boyfriends but none she was serious about. She arranged to take a day off work so she could accompany Ping to the courthouse. She could see that the trial was placing an enormous emotional burden on her friend and wanted to lend her support.

* * *

Professor Guo's attempts to analyse the symbols etched onto the surface of the Oracle, had stalled. They appeared to be simple pictograms, displaying many variations on several apparently related themes. The most common symbol was a triangle, which it seemed reasonable to assume represented the Oracle itself.

But the professor's computer wasn't being particularly helpful. The symbols were nowhere near as simple as they first appeared, concealing a complexity that was as frustrating as it was unexpected.

The professor's view of history placed modern man safely atop the pinnacle of human achievement. The idea that some ancient civilisation might have developed systems of greater sophistication than whatever is required to slaughter pigs, wasn't within his intellectual paradigm.

He stubbornly refused to see the obvious until one of his students came across a printout of the symbols on his desk.

Hu Ya wasn't an average student. He was the one thing that most modern Chinese educators despise and fear, an individual imbued with intuition and imagination. He was lounging near the bottom of the tutorial in terms of his grades and the professor considered him to be lacking any aptitude for the subject.

Ancient history was not supposed to be a creative subject. It had already happened and too much interpretation of the accepted facts tended to cloud the pool, resulting in unnecessary contradiction and subsequent confusion. Hu Ya appeared to specialise in both of these impediments to clarity and insight.

He noticed the symbols and the computer's interpretation on Professor Guo's desk as he was handing in an assignment. He was intrigued. Immediately he recognised that they were listed in the wrong order. They had been listed according to their complexity and this rendered the sequence meaningless. Hu Ya was able to reposition most of them to produce a pattern. He respectfully asked the professor what the intriguing symbols represented.

Professor Guo was nearing the end of a long day and was in no mood for the ill considered comments of a below average student. In frustration he handed Hu Ya the sheet of paper and told him to take it away and come back with an analysis the next day.

"What's it supposed to be?" asked Hu Ya.

"It's a puzzle," replied Professor Guo. "See if you can discern any meaning from it."

Hu Ya worked all through the night trying to fathom his way into the mystery behind the symbols. Some of them were obvious. They were alignments with what appeared to be the moon. Others were less obvious, perhaps representing musical scales or cycles of variations of specific intervals of something.

By the next afternoon he was exhausted and finally got some sleep, with the first draft of his interpretation sitting on his desk. He awoke just after midnight, his mind flooded with symbols. After half dreaming and half thinking for an hour, he got out of bed and began scribbling frantically, consigning his previous night's efforts to the rubbish bin.

The next morning, a day late, he approached Professor Guo with his conclusions.

The professor handed Hu Ya his assignment freshly marked with a 'D'. He'd all but forgotten about giving him the infuriating symbols as he absent mindedly accepted the piece of paper his student was eagerly proffering. He adjusted his spectacles.

What he saw made him gasp. He had also spent a lot of time thinking about the symbols and immediately recognised many of the interpretations. He looked from the paper to Hu Ya then back to the piece of paper.

"Where did you get this from?' he asked in disbelief.

"I've been working on it since you gave it to me."

"This is good! How did you come up with it?"

"Once I'd deciphered the obvious, I noticed a pattern that helped me understand the rest. Is it correct? Did I solve the puzzle?"

"Do you have any idea what this is?" asked the professor.

"Some sort of instructions."

"These symbols are etched onto the outer surface of an ancient replica of the Oracle of Singh Ma."

"What's the Oracle of Singh Ma?" asked Hu Ya, mystified.

"You may have helped us unlock an extremely ancient code," said the professor, ignoring his student's questions.

"I found the symbols very aesthetically pleasing. You told me it was some kind of puzzle and I didn't want to let it beat me."

"This is amazing," said the professor.

"This isn't," said Hu Ya examining his assignment.

"Give that back," said the professor. "I haven't finished marking it."

Professor Guo took both documents and retired to his office to reconsider one in the light of the other.

* * *

That afternoon Professor Guo summoned Tashi into his office.

"I think I've managed to work out the meaning of the symbols," he boasted excitedly. "It took a lot of work but I think I've cracked the code."

"So what does it mean?" asked Tashi.

"It's a set of instructions."

"Instructions for what?"

"I'm not sure. They require the Oracle to be aligned in a very specific way during the full moon. It appears to be dependent on some kind of ancient pagan ritual. I want to try to unlock it but the next full moon isn't for another two weeks. That gives us plenty of time to try and determine what else might be required. The meaning of some of the symbols is still doubtful."

"So what do you want me to do?"

"Nothing. I just thought you should be kept informed as we make progress. You discovered it and I thought you'd be interested."

Tashi already had a low opinion of the Archaeology Department and none of this discussion was helping it to improve. He wished Ping was back from Hong Kong. This was her subject, not his. He considered Professor Guo an over excited nutcase. An ancient pagan ritual indeed! Next they'd be sacrificing chickens and chanting nonsense to some long forgotten god.

When Ping rang that night he remained unimpressed.

"Professor Guo wants to hold some kind of ancient pagan ritual," reported Tashi after Ping had summarised another dull day in court.

"How exciting," said Ping.

"You think that's exciting?"

"What do you think?"

"I think they're all mad and it's a waste of time."

"It's more exciting than sitting in court all day listening to criminals tell lies about my father."

"How's your mother?"

"Still the same. She's pretending father has gone overseas."

"We should introduce her to Professor Guo. I'm sure they'd get along famously."

"That's not very nice!"

"Sorry. I miss you! When are you coming back?"

"Soon. I'd like to be there for Professor Guo's crazy pagan ritual."

"That won't be for another couple of weeks. He's waiting for the next full moon."

"I should be back by then."

"Good."

* * *

The court case lumbered inconclusively onwards for another ten days. The only real excitement had been the day Aixia accompanied her. Every male in the courtroom turned and stared as they entered the gallery. They'd sat together and listened while Ping's father was accused of everything from cruelty to donkeys to whimsical, cold blooded murder.

Over the following days, which she endured without her friend's support, the prosecution was able to produce collaborating witnesses to confirm most of Dan Ban Ho's allegations. The defense only had Irfan to refute them. Ping felt like she was drowning in wet concrete.

Frustrated and miserable, she left the court and took a taxi directly to the airport. Aixia had been unable to keep postponing a date she'd promised one of her suitors and wouldn't be home until late. Ping was carrying most of what she needed in her handbag and couldn't face going back to the deserted apartment, just to get her luggage. Aixia could forward it or donate it to charity or whatever she wanted. It really wasn't an issue in the context of the mess her father was in and her desire to get back to Tashi.

He met her at the airport after her plane landed at Xian'yang but his joy at seeing her was soon eclipsed by fresh news of the growing hopelessness of her father's predicament.

* * *

Two nights after her return, the moon was ready to play. As far as Tashi was concerned, it could just as relevantly have been called the fool moon. He certainly felt like a fool as he and Ping accompanied Professor's Guo and Xu to a spot on top of the highest hill near the university. In his bag, Professor Guo carried the Oracle, freshly retrieved from the Archaeology Department's safe.

In Tashi's opinion, Professor Guo was committable. He'd crossed the final frontier that separates the inspired enthusiast from the total freak. Professor Xu was slightly less crazy. His enthusiasm was less manic and he managed to exude a slight air of intelligent authority that was completely lacking in his colleague.

Ping was happy for any distraction from her family's percolating problems.

Professor Guo practically danced to the summit only to find it inhabited by pairs of students attempting to share private romantic moments. The last person they wanted to invade their foreplay was some nutty professor on a mission of historic enlightenment. They were dispersing as Ping, Tashi and a slightly asthmatic Professor Xu attained the hill top.

It was a beautiful night, the stars shone like freshly invented equations on a virgin blackboard.

The moon had ample radiance for every worldly purpose, including both the insane and the lusty.

Tashi was neither. Ping was a little of both and Professor Guo was off any measurable scale. Professor Xu simply appeared old and unwell.

Besides the rustling of trees in the breeze, the only sound was Professor Xu's wheezing as he sat down, lit a cigarette and sucked the smoke into his lungs as though it contained some magical elixir.

The Oracle glistened with an other-worldly sheen as the moonlight appeared to recognise and caress its infrequently exposed surfaces.

Professor Guo excitedly produced a compass. The moonlight was sufficient for him to determine north and he desisted from producing the bulky flashlight he had carried with him.

Tashi was already bored. Ping was desperately spanning two irreconcilable worlds hoping they wouldn't spin away to opposite ends of time and space.

The Oracle sat stubbornly in the moonlight, refusing to be anything other than a scientific embarrassment. Professor Guo attempted several realignments but nothing triumphantly paraded before the full moon.

"Maybe we need to slaughter some chickens," suggested Tashi.

"What?" wheezed Professor Xu.

"I think he's getting hungry," attempted Ping.

"Food? How can you think of food at a time like this?" demanded Professor Guo.

"Sorry," said Tashi. "I'm a dentistry student and I was just trying to include something I can understand."

Ping shot him a look that even in the moonlight would have resulted in a perfect strike had her eyeballs been of the bowling variety.

"We must have misinterpreted some of the symbols," sulked Professor Guo, suddenly regretting his reliance on the conclusions of a D-grade student.

"Maybe they don't mean anything," suggested Tashi. "Have you noticed that there are three different ways the two halves can be put together?"

"Two halves? What do you mean?" asked Professor Guo.

"It's made up of two pieces. Let me show you," said Tashi using the same tone of voice he would have deployed to talk to a chimpanzee.

He took the Oracle from the bewildered professor and twisted it until the halves separated.

That effectively marked the end of the night's endeavors. Neither professor had been aware the Oracle was made up of two separable parts. They'd assumed it was a solid object. This new revelation was most untimely.

Tashi reassembled it another way, recombining several of the symbols into something completely different.

"Ungh," said Professor Guo. "I can see I have more work to do. I'll need to copy the symbols from all three combinations."

"He's an idiot," said Tashi after the professors had reclaimed the Oracle and left.

"He's an expert in his field," said Ping indignantly.

"Yeah, so are cows," countered Tashi.

The next morning Hu Ya was given two new assignments.

"What's this for?" he asked.

"It's to help you develop logic. If you can solve these puzzles you'll be a far better student," claimed Professor Guo.

"Why am I the only one who's been given these assignments?"

"Do you want to pass this course or not?" the professor shot back angrily.

* * *

Irfan's leg was healing quickly. The bullet had passed through his calf muscle, just missing the bone. The only good thing about being confined to a jail hospital was that he was receiving excellent medical treatment. They wanted him to be healthy when they sentenced him to spend the rest of his life behind bars. His name appeared near the bottom of a long list of defendants and every few days he was wheeled into the courtroom to give evidence against some of the rest of them. He was in no hurry to sit in the dock. He had recognised some of the others whose fate was being determined along with his own. Most were at least as guilty as he was. In between prayer sessions he consoled himself that he was in a far better situation than everyone he'd left behind in the cave.

The hospital was the cleanest place he'd ever been. One of the nurses had taken pity on him and smuggled in some cigarettes which he hid under his pillow. He fingered the packet, desperately wanting to light one but knowing he had to wait until after the doctor made his last rounds for the day. He watched as the clock on the wall slowly laboured through another hour. It was dark outside but he had to endure a further half hour before it would be safe to drag himself out of bed and across the floor to the open window.

He thought about his wife and young daughter. How would they be coping without him to protect and provide for them? What had they heard? They probably thought he'd been killed in the cave with the rest. Surely it was more important for him to be with his family than stuck here waiting to be punished for perfectly justified acts. Acts that he'd performed with great skill and integrity. What gave them the right to judge and condemn him for choosing prosperity over hopelessness. He should be respected for choosing a more dangerous, treacherous path for the sake of his family. He'd been brave. He'd been courageous in the face of adversity. Certainly the rewards had been great but, hadn't he earned them?

He thought about the back breaking toil in the rice fields, his father's legacy to him. Day after day his older brother still diligently followed their buffalo through the mud, to earn a pittance. That was the way his family had survived for generations.

But times changed. He had seen American television. He remembered the day the first television set appeared in his village. He remembered the shiny cars and the beautiful women, the fine houses and the big cigars. The way they blew smoke in each other's faces to prove they had greater riches and more power.

Why was it so wrong to break away? Hadn't they learnt everything there was to learn about poverty and mud? It was time for change. Surely Allah didn't expect him to remain a helpless slave to the seasons forever. He had prayed five times every day, been a faithful husband and a good father. Who could presume to punish him? Only Allah had the right to judge him.

The doctor arrived in his usual flurry of self importance. Three nurses scurried along behind him. The one who'd given Irfan the cigarettes gave him a knowing wink.

They took his temperature and pulse while the doctor examined the chart at the end of his bed. Some notes were added and they were gone.

One of the nurses turned out the light.

Irfan waited until the sound of their passing receded before clutching the cigarette packet and his lighter and dragging himself painfully out of bed. He dragged himself across the floor with his injured leg hanging behind him. The brief trip to the window took him a few minutes. After pulling himself up to the windowsill he ignited his earthly reward and gratefully inhaled a lung full of smoke.

After a few minutes he heard an incongruous creaking sound as the floor boards betrayed the presence of an intruder. Irfan quickly stubbed out the freshly lit cigarette and froze.

A shadow approached his empty bed.

His eyes were adjusted to the darkness and he was able to discern a quick series of movements. There was a barely audible grunt of dissatisfaction from the intruder who then exited the room as quickly and stealthily as he'd entered.

Irfan was aware of the sound of his own breathing. He considered lighting another cigarette but his criminally honed instincts vetoed the idea and he crawled painfully back to his bed.

The sheets were slightly ripped. The intruder had used some sharp object to puncture several holes through the bedding and mattress.

Irfan was put into another ward with an armed guard at the door. That meant no more cigarettes. He was amazed that the state was prepared to invest so many resources to keep him safe just so it could eventually lock him in jail. Where had the state been when his family were starving? Why were they prepared to waste so much money on him that provided him with so little benefit? He found the entire process to be unfathomably misguided.

The Hong Kong government were little better than the godless Chinese Communist Party. They made up their own stupid rules with no regard for reality or people's needs. They had some kind of crazy agenda that was outside divine law. They were infidels and everything he saw every day confirmed that fact irrefutably. He had no doubt that whatever judgment they passed on him would be instantly overturned in heaven.

EIGHT - INSIDE THE CAGE

Hu Ya worked long and hard. The new puzzles were less fun than the first one. Had he realised that solving the first puzzle was only going to result in more puzzles, he might not have been so enthusiastic. The first puzzle had been tied in with things he could more easily understand. These next two were less enthralling.

He spent two days on one of the puzzles before giving up in frustration. He moved onto the other one, which seemed to be similar in many ways, but with variations. He couldn't imagine what all these weird symbols had to do with archaeology.

That night he had a strange dream. The symbols danced in front of him and then turned into animals and were herded into a cage. Inside the cage they turned into ants and escaped through small holes. Then it started raining and they floated away down a river. He woke up even more confused.

But suddenly it was as though the symbols had rearranged themselves. The answer was obvious. He'd interpreted one of the symbols as the sun. But if he changed that to be the person conducting whatever the ritual was, it became less complex. It gave him a point of reference to rearrange the others.

The same misinterpretation of the symbol had occurred in the other puzzle. If he applied his new idea to it, once again, it lost a lot of its complexity. It was all about simplification.

By lunchtime he had an answer. The puzzles had finally opened up.

He hadn't had much respect for the professor up until that moment, but the way these puzzles had finally revealed their beauty and simplicity forced him to reconsider his judgment. It wasn't just logical, it was beautiful. It was almost like a form of symbolic poetry.

"I don't even care if I get another 'D'," he thought happily as he wrote out the final formula, or whatever it really was.

Professor Guo was delighted. He almost smiled before his cold, detached professionalism reasserted itself. He'd also been wrestling with the 'puzzles' but hadn't gotten anywhere near to a solution. He glanced across the results of Hu Ya's hours of meticulous work.

"It's not perfect," confessed Hu Ya, believing he was dealing with a mind capable of producing a baffling but consummate masterpiece.

"You've done very well," said the professor, unable to fully contain his glee.

"It solved itself in the end. I was just lucky to be there at the time."

"Have I told you about the Oracle of Singh Ma?" asked the professor appearing to change the subject.

"I think you've mentioned it. Is it another puzzle?"

"You could say that. Only infinitely more sophisticated."

"I'm a bit puzzled out after those," confessed Hu Ya. "Maybe we could save that one for some other time?"

"Of course," chirped the professor, picturing himself accepting the accolades of an admiring academia.

"I've finished marking your assignment." He handed Hu Ya the only paper he'd ever written that received a grade above C +. Beside the crossed out D, it was clearly and unambiguously marked 'A'.

* * *

"It's a lot more complicated than I originally thought it was," confessed Professor Guo.

"In what way?" asked Ping.

"There are three different yet complimentary sets of instructions. It appears they all need to be deciphered."

"That does sound complicated."

"Exacerbated by the fact that we're not 100% sure about any of them. We can only try out the options we have. They may be partially or even completely wrong but we've got to start somewhere."

"That doesn't sound very hopeful."

"We should be able to work things out by trial and error."

"Let's hope so."

"All three sets of instructions appear to begin with physical specifications concerning the alignment of the artefact to the points of the compass and the relative position of the full moon. Then the most likely interpretation we've so far been able to come up with appears to require certain tonal inflections of sound. These are probably going to be the most difficult part."

"That's amazing," said Ping.

"It's a lot more complex than I first envisioned but the instructions appear to be consistent and I'm hoping we'll be able to make them work."

"And what's supposed to happen when we get it to work?" asked Ping.

"That's yet another mystery at this stage."

"What if it's dangerous?"

"I don't see how an ancient artefact could pose any serious threats."

"That's what they said about the tomb of Tutankhamen. Then all the people who discovered it suffered inexplicable deaths."

"I don't think there are any curses attached to this piece. It's of Buddhist origin and they don't deliberately harm anything. There's nothing here or in any of the literature that warns us of anything like that."

"I hope not."

* * *

The night of the next full moon darkened unimpressively overhead. Clouds obscured the sky as the muffled lunar disk rose above the urbanised horizon. It constituted little more than a dim glow through a congealed haze of dusk and the late afternoon rush-hour smog.

Professor Guo cursed quietly under his breath as he felt obliged to assist Professor Zhao from the music department, stumbling upwards behind him. Professor Zhao was additionally encumbered by a large saxophone. After claiming he'd deciphered what he and Hu Ya were convinced was a series of musical tones, he was officially conscripted to personally produce the allegedly prescribed sounds.

"Nearly there." Professor Guo attempted to sound cheerful.

Professor Xu wheezed his breathless concurrence from further down the slope.

Hu Ya, struggling beneath a collapsible table, was last to ascend, worried that Professor Xu might quietly die if left entirely to his own athleticism.

Tashi boycotted the event and sent Ping as his representative. His only real interest was to ensure the Oracle wasn't damaged or splattered with chicken entrails. They didn't need him and his skepticism to spoil their pagan ritual with reasonableness and commonsense.

The little procession eventually assembled on the hilltop.

Professor Guo produced the Oracle from his backpack. Thin moonlight illuminated one of its faces as he placed it on the small portable table Hu Ya had assembled.

"We'll start with the full Oracle in its entirety," announced Professor Guo. "Then if we get enough moonlight we can try the separate parts."

Nobody argued. Professor Xu gasped quietly, wishing the clean night air could grant him some respite.

The compass was deployed to meticulously align the Oracle to the four cardinal directions.

Then Professor Zhao began to blow his saxophone. It took him a few sour notes before he settled into a strangely haunting, circular melody that was both odd and yet familiar at the same time. The universe seemed to sigh and relax around them. Everyone on the hilltop felt a subtle yet profound change in the atmosphere. The wind stopped blowing and the temperature appeared to rise a few degrees.

The moon, however was above the pleasantries and optimism being evoked by the melody and remained aloof behind thick grey clouds.

Professor Guo redeployed his compass to recheck the Oracle's placement.

Ping was almost happy Tashi hadn't come. It looked as though they were going to be beaten by the weather. Professor Guo seemed determined to get some kind of result and the way things were going, her only hope of a good night's sleep was if it started raining.

Professor Zhao was an incongruous sight blowing his horn in the semi-darkness. He'd encountered some American tourists during his boyhood in Beijing, who'd introduced him to the music of Elvis Presley. This chance introduction shaped the rest of his life and was the main reason his attention had turned to the study of music. He sported a generous growth of greased back, black hair that gave him the culturally butchered appearance of being a Chinese version of Elvis.

Nothing much happened for about half an hour. Professor Zhao continued to produce the sweet, haunting melody as Professor Guo fussed around, attempting to display academic detachment, in reality fearful of another failure.

Professor Xu sat, smoking and wheezing.

Hu Ya fidgeted. He was happy he'd been included as a reward for his contribution but found the practical part of this assignment a lot less stimulating than the theoretical side had been.

Then, almost grudgingly, in a belated demonstration of sympathy for the endeavors of humanity, the moon shone through a hole in the overhead cloud blanket.

The light struck the top of the Oracle, producing a smoky image which danced with Professor Zhao's notes. The image began to shimmer and grow until it was projected almost a metre into the night air.

Suddenly a face appeared. A smiling female face was joined by several other smiling female faces, all with silver scarves around their heads. They were some kind of hologram, somehow being stabilised by the noises emanating from the saxophone.

Ping wished Tashi was here to see this, to show him he had found something amazing.

The smiling faces in the hologram faded. A commentary began in some utterly foreign language, utilising the notes being played on the saxophone. The voice producing it was most likely masculine in contrast to the faces, which were definitely female. As the commentary continued some kind of flying ship producing its own sweet sound appeared to take off from a futuristic city. It ascended almost vertically, leaving whatever planet had produced it, and headed out towards the stars. The familiar face of the moon flashed past as it continued on its voyage out into space. What followed almost looked like a tourist guide, showing peculiar hotel rooms amongst landscapes on alien planets.

Then the clouds moved in. The whole scene disappeared as the full moon was obscured.

"What was that?" asked Ping almost as if she expected somebody might have an answer.

Professor Guo was in a state of shock. Professor Xu had actually risen to his feet and continued to stare at the space above the Oracle.

Professor Zhao was so mesmerised by the melody, he kept playing. A sudden flash of moon light reinvigorated the scene dancing above the Oracle. The 'commentary' began again as another scene struggled to come into focus, revealing another futuristic urban setting. Then the focus moved to show what looked like a cactus plant which then morphed into a lizard and then into a dinosaur.

Dense cloud obliterated any hope of further moonshine and after a few minutes rain set in. Professor Zhao stopped blowing his saxophone and ran for shelter with Ping and Hu Ya. Professor Xu walked calmly and thoughtfully behind them.

Professor Guo was the last to notice the rain. Reluctantly, he retrieved the Oracle before absent mindedly deploying his raincoat. Besides being wet, he was elated. They had partially reactivated an ancient artefact which appeared to show technology at least as advanced as their own. In fact, the way it had been engineered to be activated by the moon and sounds insinuated it was vastly more advanced.

He ran down the hill, determined to report what had happened to the authorities as soon as possible.

* * *

"It produced some kind of hologram," reported Ping after she managed to track Tashi down the next afternoon.

"Hologram? What are you on about?" said Tashi who considered anything less than a full planetary invasion an inadequate excuse to interrupt his game of chess.

"It produced some pictures and sounds. It projected them into the space above the Oracle."

"What?"

"The Oracle. It projected pictures and sounds up into the air."

"Can't we talk about this after my game?"

"No! This is important!"

"OK. Stop poking me!"

"It was like a movie being projected into the air above the Oracle. It was incredible!"

"I find that hard to believe. I'm sorry," said Tashi to his opponent. "She's not normally like this."

"Trust me! I was there. I saw it with my own eyes. Professors Guo, Xu and Zhao as well as Hu Ya all saw it. We all saw it!"

"So what did it do?"

"We didn't see it all and it was in some strange foreign language. But what we saw was really amazing. We saw faces and a spaceship travel to settlements on other planets. We saw some lizards and cactus and some other weird stuff. It was truly amazing!"

"I had this incredible dream too. I dreamt that a little pink dog came and ate the university."

"Don't be silly. This was real. You've discovered something unbelievable!"

"Yeah, I don't believe it," said Tashi moving his bishop.

"How can you be so infuriatingly normal all the time?"

"Normal people don't think being normal is infuriating."

"What's that supposed to mean?"

"It means we'll talk about it after I've finished this game and when you've calmed down."

"I'm not going to calm down!"

"Checkmate!" said Tashi taking his opponent's queen with his rook. "All right then, let's go somewhere quiet where you can tell me all about it."

Unfortunately the concept 'somewhere quiet' cannot by definition include anybody as excited and agitated as Ping and in the end they settled on somewhere noisy. They sat near an erupting fountain as jack hammers and cranes worked to construct more university buildings nearby.

"The moon was behind the clouds but when it came out the Oracle came alive in the moonlight. There were these smiling faces and then we saw some kind of space ship and then the clouds came back and it stopped for a few minutes. Then the moon came back out and it started showing us some weird picture like a movie."

"That's really fantastic!"

"Arrghhh!! Sarcasm doesn't suit you. If you must humor me, at least try to be funny."

"Funny? I was just trying to match your level of enthusiasm. You're the funny one!"

* * *

That night, most of the university awoke to the sound of sirens in the early hours of the morning. The sounds didn't last long enough to keep them awake for much longer than it took Tashi to complain about being woken up in the middle of the night.

Next day!

It began with somebody knocking vigorously on Ping's door. She opened it to find Professor Guo. He was agitated. His eyes were wide open and for almost half a minute he stood silently at the door.

"Good morning," said Ping.

"No, it's not good," said the good professor.

"Oh," said Ping unsure of how to respond.

"The Archaeology Department building burnt to the ground last night."

"What?" said Ping.

"Can I come in?"

"Of course," said Ping.

"There was a fire."

"I heard the fire engines in the night. What happened to the Oracle?" demanded Ping.

"The Oracle is here," said the professor producing it from his bag.

"The safe containing it was one of the only things that survived the flames," he continued as Ping took the Oracle from his trembling hands.

"It seems to be alright," she said.

"I've examined it and it appears to have escaped being damaged," agreed the professor.

"What caused the fire?" asked Ping.

"Nobody knows yet. There'll be an investigation of course."

"Of course," said Ping.

"I have no alternative but to return this to you," said the professor. "Please keep it in as safe a place as you can. It is a unique and I suspect, extremely valuable artefact. I know it belongs to Tashi but I feel it will be safer here than in his dormitory. I want to attempt another activation, when the moon is full again."

"Let's hope the weather is more cooperative next time," said Ping.

The distressed professor managed only a faint smile.

"I'll see you later today on campus," he said wanly as he left.

* * *

The campus was buzzing with an unfocussed sense of excitement. It wasn't just the fact that the archaeology building was a damp pile of ashes. Even Tashi could smell the tension through the aroma of fresh smoke as he made his way to his first lecture.

Fifteen minutes into it, there was an interruption. It consisted of Professor Guo, Professor Xu, and Ping. They hadn't suddenly developed some latent interest in dentistry, they were on a mission. He was their target and he could tell from their combined body language, he had no option other than to allow himself to be prized out of his seat and led away.

The little committee escorted him into a small cupboard-like office in the building next to the smoldering damp wreckage which so vividly summarised Tashi's idea of everything archaeology stood for. Tashi was offered one of the two chairs in front of the professor's hastily requisitioned desk. Ping slid excitedly onto the other. Professor Xu hovered conspiratorially behind them, billowing smoke like a coal fired power station.

Professor Guo hadn't slept. His normally disheveled demeanor was playing host to a whole new level of personal neglect. He was wearing the same clothes he'd been wearing the previous night and Tashi suspected, most of the previous week. They looked fresher than the rest of him.

However, in his eyes was a glint. He was visibly excited far beyond the call of duty which even the destruction of his entire department should have elicited.

"The artefact appears to be an ancient technological device," he began.

Tashi sat and waited, hoping he might be about to hear something he cared about.

"It seems to contain some kind of message. Our last attempt managed to partially activate it. The result was astounding. I've never seen anything like it, anywhere before."

"So I heard," said Tashi.

"The loss of the building is a major obstacle but I'm determined to persevere. We lost almost everything last night except the artefact. It was almost as if all possible distractions from this one vital project were removed. Fortunately nobody was injured and we are looking for available space on or near the campus to resume our normal lecture schedule."

"So normal lectures will be continuing?" asked Ping.

"Not this week unfortunately, but I expect the department will be back in business, as it were, sometime within a week or so."

"Speaking of which, can I get back to my lecture now?" asked Tashi.

"Yes, of course," said Professor Guo. "I'm sorry to have interrupted but I thought you should be formally informed about our latest discoveries. The loss of the department building has nothing to do with you, obviously, so I won't waste any more of your time."

Professor Xu who had remained silent throughout, attempted to flatten himself against the wall so Tashi could squeeze past. It was a futile attempt and Tashi was forced to rub against him as he escaped from the smoky den.

"I don't think he understands the significance of what he found," he commented after closing the door behind Tashi.

NINE - JUDGEMENT DAY

Yu Dong sneered at the gallery. His features contorted naturally into a smug mask of indiscriminate disapproval. The prosecuting lawyer didn't like people. He preferred cats. Cats never pretended to be anything other than cats. They were straight forward animals who knew what they wanted and didn't bother pretending things were otherwise.

Ping's father gazed out hopelessly across the courtroom.

He searched the gallery for a familiar, friendly face. There were none. Ping obviously hadn't received his urgent messages or had been unable to respond to them. His business associates and so many people he'd thought were his friends, were all too traumatised by the mere mention of the word heroin, to show him even a shiver of the support he so desperately needed. Nobody!

He didn't expect to see his wife.

He recognised Irfan across the courtroom amongst the horde of liars and wondered what had possessed this man to contradict the script they'd witnessed being enacted during the trial. He'd been the only one who'd said anything that was true.

Yu Dong was sure he could smell urine.

The judge raised his false wooden gavel and slammed it down onto the false wooden bench. The crack echoed around the room drawing everyone's attention to him.

"This court is now in session."

The case had not gone well. Being innocent proved to be a huge disadvantage. The guilty all knew exactly what was happening and had been making plans for this eventuality for years. The first he knew about this gang of drug smugglers was when the police had broken down his door. Then suddenly he was expected to defend himself from something he knew nothing about. His lawyers had done their best but ultimately had nothing to work with besides one witness whose story contradicted everything everyone else had said.

The court officials looked bored as the Judge began his summation.

"…. Guilty!"

"….25 years."

That was all he heard.

Like other innocent men, naturally he had considered the possibility he might be found guilty, but never seriously imagined a guilty verdict was possible.

With less ceremony than accorded the opening of a packet of potato chips, the once respected businessman was escorted down into the dungeons beneath the courthouse.

Irfan was stunned.

So this was their idea of justice! Jail an innocent man and set the guilty free.

Irfan was in the same group with Dan Ban Ho scheduled to be judged and sentenced the next day.

His leg was aching and the pain stopped him from speculating about how long he was going to be in prison.

* * *

Ping arrived home to find a telegram marked urgent sitting in her mail box. A telegram? She'd never received one before. She ripped it open and ingested the message. It was from Sun Xuefa, her father's lawyer.

She turned on her phone and ignoring the blast of messages and missed calls, tried to phone her mother. The number rang out.

* * *

Professor Guo was a man possessed. He'd never even dared to dream about a situation like the one he was in. He was about to rewrite human history, reversing every theory about its origins ever postulated. And they'd probably discovered a new technology so advanced it would revolutionise the future as well. He was about to fill a lot of space on the stage of world history.

Professor Xu could see that his younger colleague was undergoing a psychological melt-down. The suspension of normal university activities following the destruction of the Archeology Department was probably fortuitous for Professor

Guo. He was clearly having difficulty assimilating the information revealed by the Oracle.

Professor Xu had also sat up late into the night, filling the university's library with smoke as he searched for anything relating to the Oracle.

The Oracle of Singh Ma was considered by most of the acknowledged experts to be a legendary, mythical symbol. Nobody ever seriously expected it could or might exist somewhere in a tangible form. Even as a symbol its meaning and significance were almost entirely unrecorded. The few references he found were incomprehensibly esoteric .

This intriguing, though not inherently fundable facet of their discovery was the reason why he'd accepted the title archaeologist. It was the reason why he was fat and why his marriage had failed. Professor Xu had found the answers to all of the mighty questions he'd been too scared to ask.

It had always been his dream to find something so old, it would prove to be new.

* * *

Ping was completely stunned when she heard the verdict. She finally managed to get a call through to Sun Xuefa, a man she'd known as a family friend since she was a child. One of the reasons why she'd chosen to study in Xian'yang was because it had an international airport, a 20 minute taxi ride from her flat. She boarded a plane to Hong Kong later that afternoon after leaving a discordant blues note for Tashi at his hostel.

Alone in his cell, her father looked like an eroded pebble.

When his eyes met his daughter's they were filled with shame and confusion. Ping wanted to give him a hug but wasn't permitted beyond the bars that separated them. She didn't want to cry. She wanted to be strong and let him know she still believed in him. But despair swept all aside and she couldn't contain the sobs that were queued up inside her chest.

There was nothing to communicate. They both felt the same sense of disbelief, hopelessness and shame.

A guard led her away.

Out in the jail's front office sat two men whom she recognised from the gallery in court. One of them approached her.

"I'm so sorry to hear about your father," he said gently. Ping fell to her knees sobbing. The man attempted to comfort her while his friend retrieved her handbag from the floor. Ping was too distraught to notice the second man attach a small listening device inside her bag. He handed it back to her after she'd managed to compose herself a few hopeless minutes later.

The two men escorted her outside the prison and one of them hailed her a taxi.

Seeing her mother was even worse. At least she'd been able to feel like she was in the same universe with her father, albeit a particularly inhospitable and thoroughly miserable one. Her mother was high on happy pills and had reverted to her girlhood, happily arranging flowers in her hospital bed.

Even Aixia wasn't able to drag her out of an un-echoing universe of screams. They spent the night together, sober and in tears.

The following day Ping flew back to Xian'yang. Tashi met her at the airport and was immersed in an emotional deluge before they'd left the terminal building.

* * *

The next full moon rose into a clear eastern sky. Tashi looked out across the city lights to the giant golden orb. It almost made the day's journey seem worthwhile. But only almost. He had spent most of the day wishing he'd never climbed Mt Luguna and never found the wretched object which was dragging him away from his studies and immersing him in something that he considered a futile, foolish waste of time.

Ping squeezed his hand affectionately as the breeze played in her thick mane of jet black hair.

"Isn't this romantic?" she whispered.

Tashi steadfastly refused to be seduced by the magic of the moment and grunted in irritation.

"Perfect conditions," remarked Professor Guo enthusiastically.

"No excuses tonight," agreed Hu Ya who'd managed to have himself included in the expedition on the basis of his previous contributions and his willingness to carry Professor Guo's bag.

Professor Xu nodded his concurrence. It had been at his insistence that they'd brought the Oracle to Xi'an. Professor Xu was not climbing any more hills. He was an archaeologist, not an athlete. He had organised access to the Xi'an Astrological Observatory roof and a film crew to capture the event. He'd also arranged the funding for the minibus that transported them, as well as their accommodation.

Including the cameraman and sound recording engineer there were 11 people on the observatory roof.

Nobody else bothered to contribute as Professor Guo produced his compass and began aligning the Oracle after Tashi delivered it onto a waiting platform. The gentle rustling of the breeze was drowned out by the sound of Professor Zhao's saxophone as he tuned his reed in preparation for the night's performance. He wore a sequined gold corset under his white suit, the nearest thing he could find to an Elvis Presley costume.

"Are we all ready?" asked Professor Guo unable to suppress the trill of excitement in his voice.

"I think so," said Professor Xu after a nod from the head camera man.

"Start recording," Professor Guo instructed as Professor Zhao began to blow the strange melody he'd been rehearsing since the last full moon.

Everybody visibly relaxed except for Tashi, who regarded the spectacle in front of him as ludicrous. In the moonlight the sight of a Chinese Elvis impersonator blowing a saxophone at the fool moon was too stupid to be comical. He felt embarrassed and wondered what the two members of the observatory staff were thinking. How could three respectable university professors allow themselves to be involved in such nonsense? One of them had even somehow arranged for the government to fund it. He was grateful none of the dentistry faculty were present. He turned away from the camera hoping nobody would recognise him.

Then suddenly he noticed something strange above the Oracle. The moonlight appeared to be condensing into a dancing effigy.

A face appeared! Then several more, all smiling. They weren't Chinese. They weren't Europeans either. They looked very foreign with pale white complexions, unusually large eyes and thick red lips. They appeared to be female with no eyelashes and fine little, up turned, pointy noses. They were definitely humanoid, but strangely bird-like as well.

The faces kept smiling as they faded away and were replaced by something slightly less unrecognisable. It was a scene that may or may not have been on Earth.

The unusually peaceful melody Professor Zhao was blowing seemed to morph into other noises in the same way the moonlight had morphed into the faces. A deep male voice began to speak. Tashi assumed it was speaking but couldn't recognise any of the sounds as any language he had ever heard before. Then, inside the dancing apparition, a shiny, silvery thing left the ground and flew upwards into the sky. It looked like some kind of futuristic zeppelin as it accelerated out into space.

The zeppelin travelled past what was fairly obviously the moon and towards what he assumed was Mars. It landed in some kind of park, filled with weird purple and red plants. People wearing some sort of odd technology on their faces took some things from the space ship. It blasted off again and headed out into space.

After it passed the rings of what was probably Saturn, the picture moved beyond to one of Jupiter's moons. On its surface was a modular settlement, an architectural mosaic which looked like it had randomly evolved in a well shaken Lego set. The camera-eye view passed through its walls to reveal groups of the bird-like humanoid beings. The unintelligible commentary continued as the view backed out through the wall and refocused on the space ship, which was now passing what looked like a large rock floating in space with another modular structure on its surface. Once again the view passed through the wall to reveal other groups of strangely attired humanoids.

The whole picture changed, revealing a dark disk far bigger than any of the planets. The space ship then landed near another settlement.

Next the whole picture exploded and suddenly there were more smiling female faces. The commentary resumed but this time it was a solemn, haunting woman's voice. Cacti-like plants were clearly visible, until they morphed into a life-form which looked like something between plant and animal. Before his eyes the animal plants evolved into a lizard and then into several types of dinosaur.

Then there were all sorts of odd looking devices that emitted a wave of energy that moved outwards, striking other devices which started to move. Several of them appeared to be household appliances producing food for consumption by more proto-humans. Silver fabric emerged from one of the devices which then clothed an entire family.

The smiling female faces reappeared. They were joined by two hooded male figures. Everything else disappeared leaving the two hooded males. They looked like monks in silver suits made from the same fabric which had clothed the families. These two males also had abnormally large eyes and funny little pointed noses and appeared agitated, waving their arms around and gesticulating wildly as they spoke.

Then they produced the Oracle and waved it around as they continued to speak. There were miniature explosions of multi-coloured light. Next the view moved into the Oracle itself, like it had with the structures on the other planets. He could now see inside it.

There followed a kaleidoscope of evolving machinery, as if he was being dragged through a museum of technology. They skipped steam engines and vehicles propelled by internal combustion and went straight into futuristic rocket technology that Tashi did not understand, only to then leap into a techno-fantasy entirely beyond his comprehension. Eventually the voice stopped talking and the images faded.

Nothingness; the space between the gasps of a newly debatable reality.

"Holy shit!!" exclaimed Tashi. "What the hell was that?"

Ping threw her arms around him and kissed him before he could say any more.

"Did you get all that?" asked Professor Xu, desperately fumbling for a cigarette.

The recording engineers just stared.

"What?" said the sound engineer.

"Yes, I got it all," said the camera man, realigning himself to a reality familiar to him.

"Fantastic!" whispered Professor Guo. He was silently weeping. His tears flowed down his cheeks and dripped onto his black, unpolished shoes.

TEN - SILENT INVISIBLE TERROR

Irfan's leg was healing. It wasn't quite as good as it had been before the legal system deemed it targetable, but it was good enough. He walked with a cane as he was led into the courtroom for the last time.

His fate had been decided and he was about to be informed about their plans for his future. He expected this to be his last excursion from jail for a very long time. He gazed around the room, devouring the colours, smells and sounds he knew he wouldn't be experiencing once the prison gates finally clanged shut behind him.

He was in no hurry.

Irfan finished the prayer he was reciting and very slowly rose to his feet when commanded to do so by the translator. The translator looked almost as smug as Yu Dong as he prepared himself to butcher the Kashmiri language once again.

"Shoo shay shee shay shar," Irfan heard the judge say. This sparked up the translator who began to babble his idea of Kashmiri legal jargon. After a preamble of unfathomable legal noise, something completely unexpected occurred. Amongst all the other allegedly Kashmiri words the translator was dryly spewing forth, Irfan heard two he understood. They were, 'charges' and 'dropped'. Dropped!?! Charges?!?

He interrupted the translator, who hated being interrupted. After attempting to ignore Irfan the man finally spat, "Yes! He said 'all charges against you have been dropped.' It means you'll probably be going home."

Irfan's confession had been rejected. The court had decided not to accept his truthful testimony, preferring Dan Ban Ho's lies. He hadn't expected any justice but he had expected they would apply the law. He was a drug courier! He'd confessed that he'd been doing it for years. Surely all these over-paid people were capable of a more reasonable outcome than this. Irfan stood in the dock shaking his head at the judge. He hadn't even considered the possibility that he might be set free and was in a state of shock.

One of the court attendants took his arm and led him towards freedom. Freedom? Dan Ban Ho, who had also been set free, was out there somewhere, waiting for him. The difference was that Dan Ban Ho really was free. He was free to do whatever he wanted and Irfan could easily imagine the sort of things he would be wanting to do to him.

His initial disbelief morphed through a spectrum of possibilities, all involving fear. Fear managed to contain him for quite a few seconds before he was catapulted, hopelessly, irrevocably, into a cold vault of abject terror. Had he imagined for one second that Dan Ban Ho was going to be set free, he would never have told the truth. He had thought the court and all its pretentious processes were above the criminal mess they were supposed to be unravelling. He had naively believed in justice, and believed it to be in his best interests to cooperate. And he had expected to spend the next few years safely behind a thick stone wall in a small cage with bars on the door and window, secure in the clockwork delivery of three meals each day and a bed and a change of prison uniform once a week.

Irfan was escorted out of the back of the courtroom, into a corridor which led to an outer office. He could see sunlight. He'd almost forgotten how exquisite sunlight was.

Allah had saved him! Halelujah!! Praise be to Allah!

But his next thought followed all too quickly: "Why has Allah been so cruel as to cast me out from safety?"

Irfan advanced through the bureaucratic check-out-of-jail procedure like a zombie. He was authentic living dead with less chance of getting across the road outside than a legless chicken. Even if he was only one tenth the target he felt he was, he was already dead.

What was he going to do? Where was he going to go? No point trying to go home. Besides the fact that it was practically on the other side of the planet, somehow managing to get there would only share the immediate danger with his family. Maybe he should kill himself and save Dan Ban Ho the bother.

He stepped out into the sunlight. He braced himself. No shots. No knives or clubs. He turned left for no particular reason. A moving target is harder to hit. He might as well make the hit-man earn his fee.

He walked two blocks. No shots, knives or clubs. What was wrong with them? Were they teasing him?

He arrived at a park. Its greenness and the obtuse angles of the vegetation attracted him in. He'd never been in such a large city before and immediately felt slightly less uncomfortable once he was surrounded by trees. After seating himself on a bench he began to pray.

A few pious moments passed before a thought flashed into his devoted mind. The girl in the gallery! Everyone in the dock had noticed her and the rumour was that she was the daughter of the businessman Dan Ban Ho had set up to take the rap. She'd been in court when he testified. She'd smiled at him and definitely wasn't part of Dan Ban Ho's web of lies. She was the only person he knew of who might have an interest in the truth. Everyone else was happy to watch an innocent man take their punishment for them.

Irfan knew he must find her. Somehow, she was the key to any hope he had of a future.

Where to start? He looked around the park. How to find this one young woman in the vastness of a city that towered over the trees around him?

Irfan began to pray again, allowing his agitated mind some respite from the quandaries which kept threatening to swallow him.

* * *

Dan Ban Ho was furious. He summoned the three culprits into his office.

"Where is he?" he asked reasonably.

Everybody knew exactly who he was referring to.

"I'm sorry, sir. He managed to escape."

"How did he manage that?"

"We were waiting for him outside the courtroom but he must have used a side door."

"Why weren't you waiting at the side door?"

The old criminal paused. He'd assigned the task to his son-in-law. He'd thought it would be an easy assignment for Kim but Kim had not only betrayed him, he'd betrayed his daughter and dishonored the whole family by being with a mistress when he was supposed to be working.

There was a lot of blood. The old criminal clung defiantly to life and bled for several minutes.

His two underlings were made to watch. It was a brutal lesson that neither would ever forget.

* * *

It took Irfan most of the next month to find Ping. After he finished his prayers in the park, he returned to the court. A disjointed conversation of hand signals and occasionally understood words with one of the clerks who had witnessed the trial and remembered him, resulted in his grateful possession of her father's address. This was accompanied by more hand signals and non-linguistic noises which in English are referred to as directions.

Having no money meant walking. It was late afternoon and Hong Kong was braced for the frantic population swell its streets endured as the towering offices released their occupants at the end of the working day.

Fortunately the mansion was less than four kilometres from the courthouse. Unfortunately most of that was uphill. Irfan didn't mind mountainous terrain but found it difficult to comprehend why anyone would want to build a city on the side of a mountain.

The clerk at the court had written an address on a piece of paper. Irfan was able to wave it in front of a few random passersby, thereby confirming his course and receiving directions onward.

The street leading to the mansion looked like something he'd only ever seen on television. There was a red Porsche and several Mercedes parked outside enormous walled palaces. He strolled past a Bentley and a bright yellow Ferrari.

At the house, Allah blessed him with a Kashmiri security guard who was able to tell him Ping's full name and the University she was attending. The guard also gave him some food and allowed him to sleep in the deserted mansion. Inside, another blessing. Allah be praised and blessings upon the holy name of our beloved Prophet. Inside a drawer, Irfan found a few pieces of jewelry the police had somehow overlooked. He knew it was the hand of God. He gave thanks until he lost consciousness.

After a night's sleep, where he was ushered through several realms of heaven by his own beloved Jillah, his virtuous wife, he felt much better. He left the mansion, profusely thanking the security guard, and made his way down the hill, back to the city's commercial center. He was able to sell some of the jewelry to a street vendor for enough money to buy a train ticket.

Once on the train he relaxed. The journey to Xi'an took two days. The passing countryside had a soothing effect on his jittered nerves. He was glad to be out of the city. Why would anyone want to live on the side of a mountain? There appeared to be enough wealth in Hong Kong for them to be able to build their magnificent city wherever they wanted.

The entire experience bewildered him. Why had these finely attired people, with running hot water and seemingly infinite power and wealth, completely contradicted their own laws? How could they accept his solemn confession and then ignore it?

Infidels!

He avoided eye contact with the other passengers but during the morning of the second day, a small boy approached him and began talking. The child's innocence was compelling and soon Irfan was playing a hand clap game he himself had learnt as a child. The boy's mother smiled from kindly eyes, happy to see her son distracted from the monotony of the train journey. It wasn't long before the three of them were playing the game together. For the first time in many months Irfan actually laughed.

Eventually the train pulled into Xi'an railway station. The boy and his mother had ended their journey earlier that afternoon and left Irfan feeling recharged, a lot more positive about his prospects than he'd felt since long months before.

Xi'an was another bustling city. He was nearly run over by a bus as he attempted to cross the road outside the bustling railway station. Its driver blasted him with its horn as the fume spewing behemoth rumbled past. It was a timely reminder that he was as far from safety as he was from the slow moving oxcarts of his village.

He still had some jewelry left. Hunger impelled him to the nearest street stall where he was able to swap the rest of it for money. He devoured a large plate of vegetables and rice. As he ate, he stared longingly at the succulent roasting chicken and pork pieces on the grill and wondered at the thoughts of the wriggling scorpions, impaled twelve to a stick awaiting immersion in boiling fat.

It was late in the day but he wasn't tired. He had another train to catch from another station. Once again he relied on his proficiency at hand gestures and pigeon Chinese to secure directions.

After less than twenty minutes on a modern, clean inter-city express, he was in Xian'yang.

The Institute of Tibetan Nationalities in Xian'yang was only a few minutes walk from the railway station. Irfan felt intimidated by its formidable, modern architecture as he approached the campus. There was an unfamiliar smell of paper and starch mixed with several other aromas he didn't recognise. The campus itself was infused with an aura of youthful purpose as waves of students scurried between the tall granite clad buildings. Irfan felt like the only stationary point in a raging torrent of human endeavor. Where to begin? He knew he would recognise Ping when he saw her but what were his chances of randomly encountering her here? Nil? Or even less?

Prayer! He must petition Allah. With Allah's help he couldn't fail.

He spent the night curled up in one of the many doorways the university offered its temporary inhabitants. He wasn't alone. After the sun set, the city's homeless filed in to claim most of the other semi-sheltered orifices the university's architects had unwittingly provided for the city's dispossessed.

Irfan awoke at dawn. His bad leg ached from its long contact with the cold stones. Undeterred, he began his morning prayers as the homeless peeled themselves away and disappeared back into the city.

Soon the campus was alive with chattering students. The door behind him opened and he was uncompromisingly advised to relocate immediately.

* * *

A few kilometres away in a minibus heading back to Xian'yang, nobody said anything. Every ten minutes or so, somebody would think of something to say and mouths even opened in anticipation of the production of sound but words remained disincarnate. Modern Chinese vocabularies weren't able to provide even an introductory syllable capable of approaching the wonder and awe that flooded the amazed minds stalled at the threshold of language.

Sleep? Oh yes! May our adrenalised, wonder infused brains please just join with the darkness one more time! Everyone had had the opportunity for a good night's sleep but they were so excited most hadn't managed to keep their eyes closed for more than a few minutes.

Tashi spent the night wondering if his mental faculties were reliable. He had witnessed something that failed at the gates of comprehension.

Ping was the only one who slept. For her the entire event was an affirmation. Her relationship with Tashi had developed another dimension of international significance. They really did have something unique and incredible that neither of them separately would have been capable of realising. Without her intervention, Tashi's half of the Oracle would still be in his parent's attic and the rest of it would still be buried in the charred wreckage where his childhood friend had died.

Professor Guo was numb. He had never actually expected to uncover anything original or significant during the course of his academic career. His drift into teaching had been a surrender to his mother's desire to produce a son whom people would admire and respect. Suddenly his obeisance had yielded a discovery beyond his wildest imaginings. He sat quietly considering possible titles for the textbooks he would inevitably be called upon to write.

Professor Xu sucked his way through a full packet of cigarettes as he stared quietly out of the minibus window. Had his smile been any bigger, it might have decapitated the top of his head.

Professor Zhao sat up the back quietly humming the melody he'd played the previous night on his saxophone. At last something had happened in his life that would even amaze Elvis Presley.

Hu Ya was blown away. He hadn't expected anything from Professor Guo, whom he'd considered a useless geek until he produced the puzzles. And now these archaeologists, these boring old men who study ancient rotting stuff, had actually come up with something that could change the whole world.

Soaring high above, a lone eagle watched as the minibus negotiated a particularly treacherous bend. Ahead was an obstacle.

The minibus rounded the bend and stopped abruptly. Nobody expected a road block, least of all one manned by uniformed soldiers, one of whom was approaching.

"Who are you and where are you going?"

"We are returning to Xian'yang, to the Institute of Tibetan Nationalities," the driver replied, confident this information would soon have the road cleared.

Suddenly, the van was surrounded by armed men.

"Everybody out!" This was clearly not merely a suggestion.

"What's the problem?" asked Professor Guo as several automatic weapons were leveled at his head.

"Out! Now!" The order was repeated several times in rapid succession.

"What's happening?" demanded Ping.

"Just do as they say," Tashi answered, squeezing her hand in an attempt to transmit a reassurance he himself did not feel.

High above the eagle watched as the minibus disgorged eight confused, protesting people. They were immediately surrounded and pushed roughly away from the minibus.

"Where is it?"

"Where's what?" The second question resulted in a rifle butt to the head of Professor Guo, who fell to the ground, bleeding. Ping tried to go to his assistance but was blocked by another rifle butt. Fortunately this wasn't applied as forcefully as the one that had downed the professor. He was conscious and producing a reasonably serious torrent of blood from a cut above his now swollen left eye.

Meanwhile some of the men boarded the minibus. After less than a minute one of them emerged, triumphantly brandishing the Oracle of Singh Ma.

After a cursory examination their leader smiled.

"Get back in the van!" he commanded.

"Give that back!" demanded Ping before Tashi could get his hand across her mouth.

The soldiers' leader frowned impatiently, highlighting a scar running down the wrong side of his face.

"Your choices are very simple," he said calmly. "Either you get back in your van and go home or we shoot you. Now, what's it going to be?"

Academics have always been renowned for their debating ability. Entire academic careers have been founded on the ability to provide a cogent, quick-witted response. However, on this occasion nobody felt inclined to present even the most rudimentary argument. Even Ping declined to respond from behind Tashi's tight grip. She and Tashi helped the still groaning, bleeding Professor Guo to his feet and accepting the futility of further protest, climbed silently aboard the minibus.

They returned to their seats and stared blankly out of the windows. The road block was pulled aside and they were sent on their way.

The rest of the journey home was awful. Once again nobody spoke, only now they were dumb from horror and shock.

Professor Guo sobbed quietly to himself. Ping attempted to comfort him but was waved away with such petulant venom she didn't bother again. Besides, he'd bled all over her handbag, effectively destroying any chance it might ever have of again being considered a fashion accessory.

They had been robbed, but not just of the Oracle, though that in itself was horrible enough. They had also been robbed of the future they were all eagerly conjuring, of their chance to ascend from mediocrity to the bright lights and glory of international celebrity.

They had also been robbed of their chance to rewrite the entire course of human history.

It just wasn't fair! Who stole it and why? How did they even know the Oracle existed?

Eventually the minibus deposited Tashi at the hostel and shortly thereafter left the rest of its stunned passengers to make their ways home from the archaeology department car park.

Once inside her flat, Ping rang Aixia and the pair spent the next two hours discussing everything from the Oracle to fingernail polish.

When she eventually got to bed, Ping tossed and turned all night.

Tashi just lay there. His mind was too tired to sleep. Nobody in the dental faculty ever got robbed. How had he got sucked into all this and why did he feel such a strong sense of loss. The stupid thing had sat up in his parent's roof for years. Nobody tried to steal it then and even if they had, he wouldn't have cared. Why, why, WHY???

* * *

Irfan managed to locate the girls' dormitory and lingered outside, watching its inhabitants come and go, hoping that amongst them he might recognise Ping.

When this failed to produce a result, he approached a young woman wearing a head scarf. Once again, he deferred to Allah, hoping a fellow Muslim would be able to help him.

The girl was from the northwestern region of Xinjiang and was a member of the Uighur ethnic minority. Fellow Muslims were rare in Xian'yang and she immediately recognised Irfan as a fellow believer by his manner and his untrimmed black beard.

She was studying the Tibetan language at the behest of her father, who believed the best hope of throwing off the hated yoke of their Han Chinese oppressors was to unite with other similarly disenfranchised peoples. Consequently, she and Irfan were able to string together enough words to invoke a rudimentary form of communication.

The girl informed Irfan that Ping was not a resident of the dormitory and offered to go to the university registrar's office to see if she could find her address for him.

By claiming to have found Ping's lost handbag, the girl was able to secure Ping's address and a hastily scribbled map, which she then handed over to Irfan.

* * *

Sleep has the disconcerting habit of tricking you into imagining it isn't going to happen just before it claims your mind. Both Ping and Tashi were surprised when they awoke. Separated by time and space, Ping was first to open her eyes to the new day. Sleep had been a blessing, a release. Being awake wrenched her back into the centre of too much tragedy for such a fine morning.

There was a weak knock at the door.

Cold, blind fear ricocheted around the room before lodging itself firmly back inside her heart. For a small regrettable moment Ping wished she was a large, formidable man.

Another, this time more forceful knocking.

Ping swallowed hard. She had several choices. She could hide under the bed and wait until the knocking stopped. She could arm herself with some item and prepare for battle, or she could simply open the door.

In the end she chose to open the door.

On the door step stood a hunched male figure. He looked like a refugee from a scarecrow convention.

"You know me?" he asked in Tibetan, polite greeting being beyond his paltry range of communicable diseases.

Ping did recognise the man. She had seen him in the courtroom where her father was so unjustly humiliated. The man standing before her was the only one in that hateful courtroom who testified that her father was innocent.

"My name Irfan," the man said. "Hong Kong," was the only thing Ping understood from the next sentence.

"Yes, yes," was all she could say in reply.

ELEVEN - ENTER THE ASSASSIN

Dan Ban Ho sat behind an enormous teak desk in his office above the discrete gold shop that was his headquarters in Shanghai. The cleaners had removed all traces of the unfortunate incident he had been forced to instigate the last time he'd been there. A gentle knock on the door caused him to wrench his irritated gaze from the computer screen in front of him and fix it threateningly on the door.

"Enter," he commanded.

The door swung inward and three triumphant men entered the room.

"We have it," said one of them bowing his head while advancing with a wooden box.

Ho was delighted. He permitted himself a rare smile, something the designer of his face had almost omitted from the plan.

The box carrier opened its hinged lid to reveal the pointed tip of the Oracle of Singh Ma.

"Excellent," grunted Ho taking the Oracle from the box and holding it up for inspection.

The box carrier placed the empty box on the desk then retreated, shuffling his two silent companions out the door in front of him.

Alone with the Oracle, Ho permitted himself an evil laugh. Happiness on the face of a man like Dan Ban Ho is an incongruous variation on the normal range of human expression. It made him look like an over-sized rat which was about to devour a cat.

He placed the Oracle on his desk and leaned back in his leather bound chair.

Eventually he leaned forward.

"Get me Phuoc," he commanded into a piece of technology that had survived for over two years on his desk.

Three seconds later there was another knock on his door.

"Enter."

Phuoc's baby face was worse than ugly. He looked like a puppy whose head had been run over several times, a gargoyle perched at the pinnacle of generations of criminality. He even smelt ugly. He was Vietnamese and had moved north with his mother after the fall of Saigon. The atrocities he'd witnessed as a child had hardened him into a killing machine. Ho cursed him with a smile.

"I want you to find somebody and deliver a message."

Phuoc grunted. An easy job and he might not have to mop up any blood. That was the worst thing about working for Ho. It always took longer to clean up the mess than to make it.

The object on the desk grabbed his attention for a nano-second of Neanderthal time. This coupled with Ho's smile made him feel uneasy.

He hesitated for a moment.

"What!?" demanded Ho, irritably sensing that his commands weren't the central issue.

"Nothing." Phuoc bowed as respectfully as it was possible for him to appear.

"This is important," said Ho. "Do not underestimate the value of the task I am assigning you."

"As you wish."

"I want you to go to Xian'yang and tell a certain young woman that I have this," he said lifting the Oracle from his desk. "Tell her I will return her property in exchange for Irfan Mullaramzan."

Phuoc could not conceal his confusion.

"If you get a chance," continued Dan Ban Ho, who didn't recognise confusion as anything he needed to deal with, "see if you can plant this bug somewhere in her flat. We had a bug in her bag but the rich little bitch threw it away. My secretary will provide you with the address and your travel documents. Now go!"

* * *

The morning after their un-triumphant return, Professor Guo convened an urgent meeting. Sitting behind his desk, his head bandaged and his eyes wide from lack of sleep, he looked like he'd been caught up in a library brawl. There were no polite greetings and no light chit chat as the victims from the minibus quietly filed in. A shortage of chairs meant Hu Ya and

Tashi had to stand while Ping and the two other professors got to sit down. Professor Guo looked as though he was about to burst into tears.

"I have reported the incident to the police," he said without any preamble. "You will all be required to provide a statement sometime in the next few days."

This was greeted with a general murmur of approval.

"I don't have to tell you how important our discovery is," interjected Professor Xu, lighting up. "We still have the footage taken on the night and are attempting to translate the audio component. I suggest we keep what we saw to ourselves until the police can recover the artefact. Without it we have no proof that the event we all witnessed took place. Unfortunately, the archaeological record is full of hoaxes and we don't want our discovery to be prematurely put into that category. Until we can be confident we can replicate what we saw, we must be very careful not to engage the skeptics."

"What if we never see it again?" asked Hu Ya.

"The police will find it," said Professor Guo without confidence.

"The Oracle of Singh Ma is not merely an artefact," interjected Professor Zhao quietly. Like all the others he had undergone a profound transformation. On this rare occasion he managed to refrain from quoting Elvis Presley lyrics. Instead he said: "It will reappear when the time is right. It's the product of forces we can neither control nor understand. The revelation we received was a blessing and it is inappropriate for us to expect or demand more."

"That may be spiritually correct," said Professor Xu exhaling a large plume of smoke. "But that's not how we operate in academia."

"How do we operate in academia?" asked Ping.

"We wait for the police," answered Professor Guo.

"That sounds like two different approaches to futility to me," muttered Hu Ya.

"Well what do you suggest?" demanded Professor Xu irritably.

"I suggest we go and have lunch," said Tashi.

All the frustration in the room was concentrated into several glares. Had glares contained ultra violet rays, Tashi would have become instantly tanned.

The rest of the meeting failed to produce anything other than futile repetition and a lot of smoke.

* * *

"What are we going to do about Irfan?" asked Ping over lunch.

"If the court didn't believe him at your father's trial, why should they listen to him now?" asked Tashi.

"Because he's telling the truth!" Ping started to cry.

* * *

Phuoc was annoyed by his current assignment. This was nothing unusual. Most of his assignments annoyed him on some level and he used his annoyance to empower him to carry them out with greater ruthlessness. But this one carried an insinuation that he found offensive, almost insulting. He wasn't an errand boy. Anyone could deliver a message to some female student at a regional university. The most dangerous part of the assignment was that it involved him. He might get bored and start killing people just to entertain himself. He had no interest in life's so called pleasures. He was only happy when he was up against a worthy opponent. He enjoyed the final stages when they begged for their life, or the lives of their loved ones. It always gave him satisfaction to achieve his purpose and end a mission quickly and calmly without emotion. He would be denied that this time. He was already irritated. There would be no closure, no finality and that meant there could be ongoing consequences.

The flight to Xian'yang was dull but quick. He was back on the ground within an hour.

To Phuoc, the streets appeared to be filled with naivety. A smug aura of comfort and safety radiated from the passers-by. Didn't these people know they could all be dead in less than the blink of an eye? There were so many of these fools, it was no wonder it meant so little whenever he snuffed a few of them out.

The funny thing was, Phuoc actually liked the Chinese. He admired the way they could flow like a stream, comfortable in a crowd. It seemed to him that the greater their numbers, the happier they were. He was the opposite. He never felt at one with a crowd.

He never felt comfortable anywhere, Why should he? He'd never taken a wife and had no family other than his mother. Phuoc was the result of an ill considered, late night, drunken encounter. His father (or more accurately; male genetic donor) had no further interest in his mother or the consequence of his speedy ejaculation and played no part in his son's upbringing. Phuoc only ever saw his father once.

It had happened during a lull in the fighting as American bombs were redirected to Laos and Cambodia in an attempt to demonstrate American contempt for the lives and well-being of South East Asians generally and to make sure that neither of these two countries got any smart arse ideas about turning communist. Phuoc was five-years-old when he and his mother boarded a bus to visit some relatives in Danang. As the dilapidated bus rattled through the countryside, avoiding bomb craters and burnt out vehicles, his mother pointed out a man sitting alone, a few seats behind them.

"That's your father."

Phuoc looked at the weather beaten old man his mother had indicated. He could see traces of his own features in the set of the man's tanned, wrinkled face. The man was gazing out of the window at the war ravaged countryside and appeared to be oblivious to the momentous fact his mother had casually imparted.

After they'd bounced a few more kilometres towards Danang, Phuoc asked his mother if he could go and sit with his father. His mother smiled and nodded her consent and the young boy made his way down the lurching aisle to the empty seat beside his father. The man continued to ignore the boy and merely grunted irritably when Phuoc attempted to initiate a conversation.

After only a few minutes the bus pulled up to pick up some more passengers. Phuoc's father stood up and pushed roughly past his son. He got off the bus and the last Phuoc ever saw of him was as he disappeared into the milling crowd before the bus resumed its journey.

Confused, Phuoc moved back to the seat beside his mother and sat silently for the rest of the trip.

Years later, he took a taxi from Xian'yang Airport. After they'd looked him over, several drivers claimed they didn't know the location of the hotel Dan Ban Ho's secretary had booked him into. Eventually he found a driver who was too scared to turn him down and they were soon speeding towards the centre of Xi'an.

The young male receptionist at the Golden Lotus Hotel knew exactly who Phuoc was as he walked into the lobby. The hotel was a tiny portion of Dan Ban Ho's real estate portfolio. A key was waiting on the reception desk and without any of the usual formalities associated with checking in, Phuoc was directed towards the elevator.

The next morning the hotel reception ordered him a taxi which took him back to Xian'yang and dropped him at the top of the street where Ping's flat was situated. He paid the fare and made his way the last 50 metres on foot.

A blind beggar with his begging bowl leaned forward into Phuoc's path. Phuoc didn't pause or break step and the bowl with its paltry contents was sent flying along the pavement. The beggar's howls of protest receded into the background as Phuoc continued towards the address written on a piece of paper in his pocket.

The door he approached was as nondescript as hundreds he'd just passed and hundreds more stretching away in front of him. The neighborhood was held together by the reluctant wealth of distant parents.

He administered what he considered to be a polite knock and waited. He knocked again. He listened for some sounds from within but was disappointed. He glanced at his Rolex. Twenty past ten. He knocked again, this time a little more insistently. Still nothing.

Phuoc didn't like being ignored. He punched the door, causing some dust and old plaster to drop, but still no reply. He grunted, turned and walked away.

Inside, Irfan sensed that something evil had touched the flat. He waited another minute and then took another breath. Whatever it was, it was gone.

But for how long? The last blow had shaken the building.

Phuoc made his way back to the hotel he'd hoped he wouldn't have to spend another night in. He stomped past reception and punched the button to summon the elevator. Fortunately for everybody else staying in the hotel, he boarded the elevator alone and endured a solitary journey to the sixth floor. He strode menacingly to his room, inserted the key and closed the door behind him. The room was comfortable and had a TV set which reconstituted satellite signals. He lay on the plush queen sized bed and manipulated the remote.

American pro-wrestling was on one of the channels. Huge muscle bound, white apes assaulted each other. Phuoc watched in fascinated disgust as they committed fake acts of over-choreographed violence, in a manner so flippant, so theatrical and so contrived, he felt personally insulted. They had replaced all the brutality, the blood and suffering of violence with show business glamour he found obscene. It was a contrived violence that failed to blacken an eye, break bones or do anything other than make its victims pull exaggerated, pained expressions. By its blatant falsehood, it trivialised brutality to the point where Phuoc wasn't even sure what he was looking at. Was this some kind of demented macho dance? Or was it just another way that corporations fooled people into handing over their money?

These people were professionals who made their living from violence like he did. But that was where the similarities ended. He wasn't an actor and nor were his victims. The blood was real and the expressions of terror and agony were genuine.

Phuoc glanced out the window. It was dark. Time to try again.

Reception called him another taxi and he was soon back in Xian'yang.

He instructed the driver to deposit him a few streets away from his destination. Students were scurrying amongst the street vendors and miscellaneous pedestrians as he retraced his steps until once again he was standing in front of Ping's door.

Before knocking he listened. Although he couldn't decipher any specific words he detected the sounds of a female voice amongst the other noises.

He knocked and waited.

The door opened, revealing a small, lavishly furnished interior and what appeared to be a very nervous young man.

"I have a message for Ping," said Phuoc.

The nervous young man looked him up and down before turning and saying: "Somebody wants to see you."

Moments later, a startled looking, attractive young woman was before him.

"Yes?"

"We have your property. You can have it back in exchange for Irfan Mullaramzan."

"Irfan Mullaramzan?"

"You know who I mean."

"Where's the Oracle?" demanded Ping.

"It's safe. Tell me where I can find Irfan and it will be returned to you."

"I don't know where he is."

"When you find out, leave a message at this hotel." said Phuoc handing over the Golden Lotus Hotel's business card. "Just tell them Irfan is waiting, They'll know what to do. You have until the end of the week."

"But what if I can't find him?"

"He'll find you, if he already hasn't." Phuoc's face contorted into the twisted imitation of a smile.

Ping shivered visibly as she closed the door.

"What are we going to do?" she said after Phuoc's footsteps had receded.

"You go straight to the police. I'll get Professor Guo," answered Tashi calmly.

"What shall I do?" whimpered Irfan.

"Hide!" they both replied in unison.

An hour later, inside the central Xian'yang police station, inspector Ding Cum leaned back in his chair and yawned.

"You must be able to do something," implored Professor Guo.

"We will do everything in our power," the inspector assured them as he wiggled his toes in the new shoes he'd just purchased that afternoon with some of the money Dan Ban Ho had sent him. "But until a crime is committed, our hands are tied."

"But they stole our property," said Tashi.

"That's an assumption. We don't know who they are or whether their alleged claim to be in possession of your property is true. All we have is your claim that something was stolen and that somebody is trying to use it as a sort of ransom."

"I want to speak with your superior," demanded Professor Guo.

"The Commissioner is on leave. I am the senior ranking officer."

"This is outrageous! I demand that you go to this hotel and arrest the man we have described," said Professor Guo.

"On what charge?"

"Theft, embezzlement, blackmail; I don't know. You're the policeman!"

"Until an actual crime has been committed, there is nothing I can do for you. Good night!"

The inspector made an exaggerated show of irritation as he pointed to the door of his office.

Professor Guo didn't bother to conceal his disgust as he followed the two young students through it.

"What are we going to do now?" asked Ping as they left the building.

"You go home and get some sleep," instructed the professor. "Professor Zhao has a brother-in-law who's an Assistant Commissioner in the Shanghai police. Leave it to me."

TWELVE - REVELATION

"We have managed a partial translation," Hu Ya exclaimed after bursting excitedly into Professor Guo's office. "The language is completely foreign. It bears no resemblance to any Chinese dialect nor any other known language."

"So how do you expect to be able to extract any meaning?" asked Professor Xu who'd been enjoying a peaceful cup of tea with his younger colleague.

"They broke it down tonally and rhythmically and fed it into a new program designed to interpret whale song."

"Are you saying it's some kind of dialect of whale?" asked Professor Guo incredulously.

"Not exactly," replied Hu Ya. "The whale song program links repeated sounds with known patterns of behavior and assumes an underlying intelligence directing the song. Whale songs are a lot simpler but the principles already discovered running through them were able to be applied to our audio recording and the result is, to say the least, very interesting."

"Ok, so what have you got?" asked Professor Xu, putting down his tea cup and placing a cigarette in his mouth.

"We have a spectrum of possible meanings. When we remove the obviously ludicrous and concentrate on the overlapping possibilities that occur throughout the spectrum, patterns begin to emerge."

"Can we begin with the most obvious patterns?" asked Professor Xu, fumbling impatiently for his lighter.

"They are the least interesting. They reduce the whole thing to some diatribe about mating and feeding. Remember this is based on what we've learned from interpreting whales."

"So you're telling us, the whole tape is worthless," interjected Professor Guo irritably.

"Not at all. At level 19 in the spectrum, the patterns congeal into something extraordinary. By level 22 they become completely meaningless."

"Are you going to tell us what you've got or not?" demanded Professor Xu through his usual smoke screen.

"Of course, but like I said, a lot of this is guess work."

"Just get on with it!" said Professor Guo.

"This is the best the program could come up with. At this level it makes the most sense," qualified Hu Ya one last time before he began to read from the transcript he was holding.

"'Greetings to our venerable descendants. If you are seeing this, either the human race and its technology have survived or some other species has attained a higher level of evolution. At this time we are not convinced that such an outcome is possible, however it is in hope of this that we have created this time capsule. Our civilisation is about to be destroyed. Our recorded history spans nearly 500 centuries and we have included an abridged version of it as part of this time capsule. During those centuries our achievements have been great. We have conquered and settled our home planet and several of the other twelve planets. Our settlers live comfortable lives at a number of locations in our Star Family. We have also colonised the great beyond of Chreznuff.'"

"What's Chreznuff?" interrupted Professor Guo.

"Other alternatives are; Chrez den, Nuffzrech or even Zedchnuff," answered Hu Ya.

"What else?" asked Professor Xu, using his cigarette to light another.

"After that they demonstrated the origins of their technology. They described some weird creature which evolved from cacti into lizards and then dinosaurs. They explained how they used the dead bodies to produce energy enabling them to produce household goods and fuel."

"Amazing," said Professor Guo.

"The narrative then went on to say," continued Hu Ya, "'This time capsule contains three parts. This, the first part introduces our civilisation and gives a general summary of our achievements. It can then be split into two separate pieces, each of which contains a different message. The parts can be accessed by treating the two halves as you have treated the whole. One half tells of our history and the factors which led to the destruction of our civilisation. The other half deals with Pyramid Asia.' There are several alternate translations of this last phrase."

"That's incredible!" exhaled Professor Xu.

Professor Guo was silent.

"Alternatively," continued Hu Ya, "it could mean 'eastern point of contact', 'triangular oriental sun dial' or 'three swirling yellow bait fish'. We decided 'Pyramid Asia' was the most likely and succinct translation."

"What could 'Pyramid Asia' mean?" asked Professor Guo.

"A lot more than three swirling yellow bait fish," answered Professor Xu.

"The final bit isn't as clear," continued Hu Ya. "They talk a lot about their technology and use technical terms we couldn't find equivalents for. Several translations below level 18 suggest that it has something to do with ocean currents and the migratory habits of squid but that's inconclusive and highly conjectural. They end by clearly stating; 'As we conclude this message, the ground beneath us is shaking and our cities are crumbling. We've used the last of our planetary defense system and a storm of meteors is rapidly approaching. Death is upon us. Soon our civilisation will be dust. If this time piece survives we implore you to learn from our folly and never unleash such a catastrophe upon Oc Thit Lip again.'"

"That's it?" asked Professor Xu.

"What do you expect after something like that?" asked Hu Ya. "It's pretty final."

"It's certainly no Hollywood ending," concluded Professor Guo.

"Do you think it could be real?" asked Hu Ya.

"What do you mean by real?" asked Professor Xu stubbing out his cigarette.

"Do you think that what it says really happened?"

"I don't know," said Professor Guo.

"How do we know it came from the past?" asked Professor Xu taking another cigarette from his packet. "It could just as credibly have come from the future."

"That's spooky," said Hu Ya.

"We should be able to get a rough idea from the positions of the stars during the journey of the space ship," said Professor Guo. "If we can determine where any particular point is in the sky, we should be able to come up with some idea of when it was or will be. The movements of the stars are predictable."

"What about the claim that the 'star family' has twelve planets?" said Hu Ya.

"Maybe it comes from another solar system," suggested Professor Xu lighting up.

"When's the next full moon," asked Professor Guo. "We need to decipher the other two parts as soon as possible."

"We need to locate them first," lamented Professor Xu.

"How's that coming along?" asked Hu Ya.

"We're waiting," said Professor Guo.

"What for?" said Hu Ya unable to contain his exasperation. His friends and he had worked night and day to produce the translation and the idea of waiting for anything made a mockery of their efforts.

"Professor Zhao's brother-in-law," replied Professor Guo.

"What's he got to do with anything?" asked Hu Ya.

"Everything, I hope," answered Professor Guo. "But don't concern yourself with that, Hu Ya. It's the business of the senior faculty."

"I think this is the business of the whole world," concluded Hu Ya.

"Exactly," concurred Professor Xu.

* * *

Three days later Professor Guo summoned Ping to his office.

"I want you to leave the message the thug wanted you to leave at his hotel. If we can lure the thieves to a location of our choosing we should be able to get the Oracle back."

"But we can't let them take Irfan. They'll kill him and he's my father's only hope of proving his innocence."

"Don't worry," assured the professor. "They may have influence with the police here in Xian'yang but they don't control the entire Chinese Police Force. We will be ready for them."

The expression of smug confidence parked across the professor's normally timid face proved contagious and Ping allowed a glimmer of hope to enter her mind.

She phoned the Golden Lotus Hotel and informed the receptionist that Irfan was waiting. She was slightly surprised when the voice on the other end politely thanked her and hung up.

When she arrived home, Phuoc was waiting on her doorstep.

Diplomacy was not Phuoc's best asset. He preferred to rip people's arms off.

"Where's Irfan?" he demanded.

"Where's the Oracle?" countered Ping.

"You will get it back when I have what I want," said Phuoc impatiently.

"I want to see it."

"It isn't here."

"Nor is Irfan."

"I will return at this time tomorrow with your property and I expect to see Irfan."

"He won't be here. Meet us next to the main fountain in the park near the university. Here's a map in case you get lost," said Ping handing him a piece of paper Professor Guo had provided. Phuoc glanced at the paper, his face contorting into a collage of barely contained rage. Without another word he turned and was gone.

Ping shivered. Her hands were shaking as she managed to get the key into the lock, opened the door and disappeared inside.

* * *

The Oracle of Singh Ma arrived from Shanghai with Dan Ban Ho the next morning. They were accompanied by two body guards and Phuoc met them at Xian'yang Airport. It was raining as they climbed into a black Mercedes and made their way to the Golden Lotus Hotel.

"As soon as you see Irfan, I want him dead."

Phuoc nodded. A kill at last. Now he understood why he was here.

"Try not to hurt anybody else. The girl's father is doing time for me so I don't want to hurt her or whoever she's with unless we have to. Just kill Irfan, quickly and then leave."

Ho left Phuoc in the lobby and took the private elevator up to the executive penthouse. It was cold and he was wet. The bodyguards following him carried a wooden box.

Phuoc went back to his room and switched on the television. It was still spewing out American pro-wrestling. Two women were in the ring. They were practically naked with hugely enhanced, barely concealed breasts welded onto their chests. They went through the motions of pretending to smash each other onto the floor, long blonde hair flying as they grunted and moaned in a pantomime of erotic dysfunction. This was an entirely new dimension in the American sport of pro wrestling and Phuoc was entranced.

There was a knock at his door. It was one of Dan Ban Ho's body guards. The other one was asleep and this one was bored. They'd been domiciled on the same floor, a few doors away and Phuoc had played cards with both to while away the hours on previous assignments. The guard had a bottle of rice wine, a beverage, somewhere between nail polish remover and Soviet era, liquid rocket propellant. Phuoc was happy to have some company. The girls had finished their violent, comedic titillation and it was back to the macho circus on TV.

By midnight Phuoc and the bodyguard, whose name was Hu, were not fit to loot a deserted church. They yelled, sang traditional songs and threw their arms around each other in gestures of brotherly intoxication and urinated on the bathroom floor.

The next morning, they were woken by the insistent ringing of the telephone next to the bed where they had both passed out. They were summoned to the executive suite.

Dan Ban Ho was under-impressed. He handed a wooden box to the body guard whose name wasn't Hu.

"Make sure you kill him," was his only comment before he ushered them to the door and indicated they should leave.

Outside a black Mercedes Benz was waiting, resplendent with smiling, uniformed door openers. Phuoc climbed in the front next to the driver.

After driving for half an hour, the vehicle stopped. Three men wearing expensive foreign suits emerged from behind its impenetrable mask of window tinting, one carrying a wooden box.

They made their way purposefully towards the fountain. The park was filled with university students and office workers on their lunch break.

Ping sat by herself.

"Good afternoon," said Phuoc. "I believe you are looking for this."

The body guard carrying the wooden box, fiddled with the latch before opening it to expose one of the peaks of the Oracle of Singh Ma.

In response, forty policemen, some uniformed and some masquerading as office workers, stormed out of absolutely everywhere. The first to arrive was plain clothed and had been lurking near the fountain. He scooped Ping up from where she was seated and carried her away from the advancing storm of authoritarian might.

Phuoc was standing beside Hu. In one movement he unsheathed his knife and pierced the heart of the nearest uniformed officer, sliced the throat of a second and lunged for the heart of another. He turned to see uniforms coming from all sides. He kicked the nearest plain clothed policeman in the chest, sending him flying backwards into several of his colleagues, a freshly drawn pistol landing harmlessly in the fountain. Then his knife was working again, red blood spraying in its wake.

Several shots were fired as innocent by-standers ran screaming from the unfolding carnage. The body guard carrying the wooden box fell backwards with blood streaming from his forehead. A bullet whistled past Phuoc's left ear as he thrust his blade wildly, splattering himself and his surroundings with blood before he hurdled some bodies and sprinted towards an adjoining park.

Hu was swamped by police and bashed to the ground. The fountain turned red as two of Phuoc's victims bled to death in the water. Several more shots were fired but the bullets failed to slow Phuoc and he sprinted through the trees, pushing terrified by-standers out of his way. Several police gave chase but Phuoc had the evasion instincts of a Houdini rabbit. He disappeared into a nearby crowd and was soon walking calmly, attempting to blend into the street scene as effectively as somebody dripping with other people's blood could.

"Where's Inspector Ding Cum!?!" demanded Hu as a uniformed officer stood on his face. "I demand to speak to Inspector Ding Cum immediately!"

The black Mercedes accelerated into the traffic as several bullets ripped through it.

As soon as the shooting stopped Professor Guo launched himself into the middle of the melee and was able to secure the Oracle. With the box in his arms the professor held on, refusing to relinquish his treasure until it was in the university's safest safe, in the administrator's office.

Ping was in shock. She'd never seen people die before. The policeman who'd carried her to safety wrapped his jacket around her as she sat shivering on a park bench.

Tashi had been waiting with Professor Guo. He took Ping's shaking hand.

Several streets away Phuoc was furious. Dan Ban Ho had assured him the police were on his payroll.

He briefly considered he'd let everybody down, but if he hadn't run, he would have ended up like the other two, either dead or in handcuffs.

How much did the rice wine affect his performance? Would the outcome have been any different if he hadn't been hungover? Besides the 40 policemen, rice wine was the only other thing that had affected his performance.

He knew he couldn't go back to Dan Ban Ho's hotel. That would be stupid.

He merged with the crowd and followed its flow for a few blocks until it thinned out and became a less than appropriate shield. He entered an eatery and made his way to the bar.

"Rice wine!"

A clear plastic bottle filled with opaque white liquid and an accompanying glass were placed in front of him. Money was exchanged. Phuoc took his purchases and retired to make a dim corner into a dark corner.

The afternoon reluctantly gave way to the evening which itself eventually gave up and finally let the night fall.

Somewhere amongst all that complicated planetary motion, Phuoc staggered back out onto the street and down several badly lit alleys until he came across a particularly rundown looking building with a sign hanging from its weathered façade claiming it was a hotel.

An old woman sitting behind the hotel's version of a reception desk accepted his money and handed over a key. She didn't bother to ask for identification.

There was no elevator and he ascended a creaking staircase to the third floor where he located a door that responded positively to the key.

The room was marginally less dirty than he was and contained a bed. On the bed was a glossy card with a picture of a partially dressed, attractive young woman. Phuoc always had extra testosterone flowing through his veins after he'd killed people. The blood lust transferred seamlessly into sexual lust and the 30 Yuan price tag above the phone number provided the final part of an irresistible equation. He fumbled through his blood splattered jacket pockets and produced his cell phone.

Less than ten minutes later, as he lay on the bed cursing every layer of the multi-faceted mess he was in, there was a gentle knock on his door. He opened it to reveal a far less attractive and much older woman than the girl on the glossy card. She smiled and opened her jacket, revealing a lot more than he had seen in the glossy picture. For the first time that day, he smiled and stepped back to allow the woman to enter his room.

Phuoc was a regular client of what he referred to as 'taxi girls'. This particular taxi was more of a rickshaw than a limousine and he could see she'd been around the block many times. However she provided him with a smooth ride, her experience produced a few short cuts and she soon had him efficiently and comfortably where he wanted to go.

Sometime in the middle of the night, Phuoc started to replay a dream he'd had many times before. It began as it always did with him playing with Van, his childhood sweetheart, in a field down by the river near the small village where he grew up. She ran down to the river picking flowers and laughing. Suddenly there was an explosion. The ground shook, knocking Phuoc onto his back. As he sat up he could hear Van screaming. She was trying to crawl towards him but the lower part of her body was a bleeding slimy mess.

He woke up. The screaming stopped. Beside him was another bleeding slimy mess but it was silent with wide open eyes and an expression of confused terror. His taxi girl looked like a rickshaw which had collided with a very large truck. Phuoc decided a hit and run was his best strategy. He washed, dressed and left.

THIRTEEN - THE NEW ANCIENT

The next full moon coincided with a clear, hot night. Professor Guo was delighted. His insistence that everybody be sworn to secrecy seemed to have prevailed.

Tashi, Ping, Hu Ya and Professors Guo, Xu and Zhao, gathered in a tea house after the days classes.

The excitement in the room was more tangible than Professor Xu's cloud of smoke. Again they traveled in the minibus, but this time they were accompanied by six well armed security guards from a private security firm employed by the university. The minibus took them to the private garden of Guan Yingpu, the Communist Party secretary for the Xi'an region. He was an old friend of Professor Xu and though skeptical of the claims, was interested to see for himself just what had got his usually calm and reserved old friend so excited.

After a grueling four hour journey, they were welcomed onto the lawn of a sprawling compound by the Secretary himself.

Two hours later they were ready. Two camera crews were set up to record the event. The Oracle was split into its two halves, one of which was selected to be activated first.

Professor Zhao began the proceedings with a variation on the notes he had played previously. A hauntingly melodic sonic code drifted into the night air. Once again everyone relaxed, the universe sighed and the temperature appeared to rise. The full moon continued its lonely journey up into the clear night sky.

An image began to appear. It was an older version of one of the birdlike males they'd seen before. Once again he began to speak in the same strange language. He waved his arms and images appeared in the air around him. At first, there were scenes of great battles being fought with advanced weaponry. Several individual faces appeared in what were obviously extremely opulent conditions. As he spoke another image appeared above him, like that of a moon but covered with somehow disconcerting, coloured pictures.

After six minutes and 20 seconds the older male sat down in a type of floating hammock. He continued to speak and waving his hand, produced images of large, crowded cities. Then he showed the face of a planet reminiscent of Earth.

Next he produced images of space ships traveling through space. The solar system they travelled through looked very different to the one containing the present day Earth. Amongst a host of more subtle differences, it held 12 planets. Only Saturn, with its distinctive rings, was recognisable. The ships originated from the third planet but then most other similarities stopped. The next planet out appeared to be green and then there was a large blue world which appeared to be entirely under water. Creatures resembling modern whales and dolphins were shown swimming beneath its waters. Next out was an even larger yellow planet. Finally the ship arrived at the 12th planet, which was purple and even larger than the star it orbited. Similar settlements to the previous scenes were shown on seven of the planets. They all appeared to have local life forms, most of which bore little resemblance to any of the living inhabitants of modern day Earth.

After some more emotional speaking and the appearance of more faces, the male speaker produced an image of what appeared to be a type of poppy flower. Then he walked through rows of waste high bushes as though he was in some kind of agricultural setting. A few seconds later the scene around him changed into what looked like some type of laboratory. After producing several types of mushrooms by waving his hand in the air, he was suddenly surrounded by fields of what looked like hemp. He spoke for a while longer before a series of other faces appeared in the air around him, each one fading away as he continued to speak.

He produced a small device which he waved around for a few seconds and then the entire scene turned into a sea of dead bodies piled up around some sort of antenna. The dialogue continued and he reappeared, seated once again in his floating hammock.

He continued to speak, producing what looked like a computer chip which then reappeared inside the brain of another male. This person seemed to be involved in some kind of mind game or hologram emitted from the computer chip. He then became very thin, turning almost into a skeleton before he dropped dead. Many other skeletal people were also shown falling down, presumably dead.

The scene returned to the lone narrator seated in his hammock. This time he conjured what looked like showers of meteorites and then an enormous space rock collided with the blue submerged planet, producing an explosion and a blast wave that almost destroyed the two planets closest to it.

This was followed by cataclysmic scenes from what appeared to be Earth, with huge waves washing over densely populated coastal areas.

Another explosion filled the sky with multi-coloured lights. The enormous outer planet disintegrated, producing another blast wave that shattered its nearest neighbor and reduced both to smoldering space debris.

Finally a comet was shown, hurtling through space towards the central star with some of the other planets in its path. Before any impact, the scene reverted to the lone figure seated in his floating hammock. He appeared to be agitated, waving his arms around and gesticulating wildly.

The entire event went for 36 minutes and 48 seconds before the figure finally faded out for the last time.

Everybody sat stunned.

Professor Guo looked around as though he'd just arrived from another universe. It took him the best part of a minute before he regained his professorial awareness of who he was, where he was and what he was doing. He held the second piece of the Oracle tightly in his grip.

He rose from his seat next to Party Secretary Guan and strode robotically to the marble plinth the Secretary had so kindly provided. He swapped the first piece of the Oracle with the piece he was holding. An unusually speechless Hu Ya used the compass to orient it in the direction the symbols indicated. He took a reverential step backwards and gave Professor Zhao a nod, signifying all was ready.

This time the notes created a melodic tune. Once again the world around them appeared to relax.

One minute passed, then two. Still nothing.

Professor Guo looked first at Professor Zhao and then at Professor Xu. Both held his gaze.

"Let's try another angle?" suggested Hu Ya. "Try turning it 180 degrees."

Professor Guo nodded blankly as he and Hu Ya made the adjustment.

Once again the enchanting melody wafted into the night air.

Another image began to appear. A blinding white light mesmerised all the witnesses. Ping closed her eyes.

Then out of the light came the image of a black crystal pyramid. It began pulsing then shrank to reveal its size as less than miniscule in the vastness of space. Then it linked up with other points of light, almost like stars, in an enormous pattern that looked like a giant glowing spider web.

In front of this appeared another presenter. This time she was a bare breasted female. All the males present gasped involuntarily when the image appeared, her large, well formed breasts, glistening with oil. She wore exquisite pink jewelry on her arms and around her neck. Even with her birdlike facial features, it was undeniable that this was an extraordinarily beautiful woman.

She began to sing a demented, discordant melody.

She stopped singing abruptly and began a dialogue.

The black crystal pyramid reappeared in her hands, its size changing to the size of the Oracle.

Three other women appeared and then two young males. Suddenly the crystal shone brightly before turning a golden colour and then became the centre of what appeared to be a map. Another 61 variously coloured triangles appeared on the map, spaced evenly across what seemed to be the surface of the planet. This was then overlaid with lines like another glowing spider web. Everywhere the lines crossed, there was a triangle.

Next appeared some shaded grey areas that didn't seem to have any specific relationship to any of the triangles. As this was occurring the commentary continued.

The map and everything except the central golden triangle faded away. The view then reoriented above the triangle, looking down onto a square with four lines emanating from each corner and intersecting at its centre, producing four new triangles of equal size.

The line at the top of the square turned gold and another commentary began. The gold colour filled the triangle, then the triangle on the left side turned purple and after several more minutes of commentary the triangle at the bottom turned red. More commentary followed until the final triangle on the right side turned blue.

Next, the original black crystal pyramid appeared and the four colours radiated up into the sky from its apex. There was a parade of happy androgynous children before the images disappeared.

Once again the female presenter held the pyramid in her hands and spoke for a few more minutes before a series of musical notes was produced by what appeared to be the rotating planet. Then the hologram faded and disappeared, leaving only the half of the Oracle which had produced it.

* * *

That night, Ping and Tashi lay on their backs in separate rooms staring at the ceiling. Elsewhere in the Party Secretary's sprawling mansion, Professors Guo, Xu and Zhao also stared at the ceiling.

Guan Yingpu, the Party secretary lay awake tossing and turning, pondering the imponderable. That meant his wife also didn't get any sleep.

Hu Ya didn't even bother to go to bed. He spent the night sitting in a chair staring at the wall.

The next morning they assembled for breakfast in an elaborate dining room. Nobody ate. Nobody spoke. Their senses had been overloaded. Even Tashi was humbled and silent, unable to find some quirky comment to kick start the conversation.

Party Secretary Guan eventually broke the deadlocked stillness by asking if anybody required any special dish for breakfast that was not already displayed on the lavishly set table around which they all dumbly sat.

Professor Xu managed to decline the offer as he fumbled for his third cigarette of the day. Everyone else either shook their heads or just stared uncomprehendingly.

Sometime later, they boarded the minibus to make the four hour return journey back to the university. The security guards had remained outside the compound and hadn't witnessed the extraordinary events of the previous evening. They barely recognised the stunned group as the same people they'd accompanied the previous day. There was no enthusiasm, no chatter, or any indication that anything other than having their tongues amputated, had occurred.

FOURTEEN - THE PAST AWAKENS

Two days later Professor Guo convened a meeting in a tutorial room near his office. Ping, Tashi, Professors Xu and Zhao and Hu Ya all shuffled expectantly into the room.

Tashi and Ping had spent most of the time since their arrival back in Xian'yang in Ping's flat. Neither were able to face mundane lectures on mundane subjects. They'd recovered from their dumbness and numbness but still spent a lot of time staring blankly at the walls. Irfan stayed inside a large cupboard in the hall, emerging occasionally to make tea. They hadn't eaten.

Professor Guo addressed the assembled group.

"I don't have to tell you that we have been privileged to witness something utterly incredible. We all saw it and looking around this room it's easy to see that we've all been changed by what we witnessed. Hu Ya has been working with the team in the languages department and they've prepared a preliminary translation. However before I invite him to read the translation, the astrologers have come up with two alternative attempts to assign a date to the revelations, based on the positions of the stars shown during the sections on space exploration and colonisation."

He paused to allow the import of what he was saying to sink in.

"According to the best astrological minds in China the artefact and the events depicted are either approximately 347,000 years in the past or they will happen roughly 220,000 years in the future."

This information managed to elicit a gasp of amazement from everyone including Tashi.

The professor sat down and Hu Ya rose to address the gathering.

"We have been able to refine our translation techniques by standardising some of the terminology from the first revelation," he began. "We've managed to come up with some possible translations for both parts of the event we all witnessed."

He began reading from the text he was holding.

"'Hello. My name is Rupkey and I am an historian. It is my regrettable duty to present for you a summary of the events that have led to the collapse of one of the greatest civilisations ever to grace the face of our beloved planet, Oc Thit Lip.

"'Infinity can be found in everything. It's a function of our human consciousness. It's where we choose to apply our attention that infinity is manifested. The more we look into something the more we find. Every aspect of this attempt to summarise our history could be developed infinitely. What follows are only the events that I have chosen to emphasise.

"'For the sake of brevity, I will focus the majority of this narration after Year One. That was the year of unification when Oc Thit Lip achieved a single world government, approximately 46,000 years ago. Before that time we existed as a number of independent states each competing for dominance and control of the planet's resources.

"'In societies based on systems of exploitation, governments go through three stages. These can take centuries or mere months to unfold. They start off by doing what needs to be done, attentively serving the will of their people. Later the state apparatus deteriorates, so that it and its members do what they want to do and whatever benefits their families and close associates. Finally, states end up spending all their time and resources trying to explain why they aren't doing what the people want them to do or simply enforcing their own will, through violence.

"'The centuries before unification were all dominated by governments enacting this predictable scenario. They were the most bloody in our history. Most of the major developments were derived from technologies designed to kill people. Unification was achieved at an enormous cost in lives and destruction, some of which continued unabated for several decades afterwards.

"'One great man united the petty national and tribal hordes of the human race behind a single banner. His name was Hudlewrink. He was the first Regent of Oc Thit Lip, and a great administrator who united the religions and codified the law. He made the peoples one.

'"Before Hudlewrink, our societies were inhibited by systems of exploitation. Greed and selfishness ruled and unscrupulous, immoral charlatans prospered and flourished. Most people were swept along by whatever form of exploitation was fashionable at the time. They abandoned their morality and dignity, to conform to whatever non-sense or propaganda they were fed by their exploiters. Empathy, compassion and generosity were considered by the controlled masses to be symptoms of stupidity. It was every individual for themselves.

'"Successful people were driven by their own personal desire for advancement, at the expense of their neighbors and anybody or anything else. This had a terrible impact on the environment and human relationships generally. Everybody was compelled to be selfish on most levels and it was reflected in all human activity from families through to nations. Husbands and wives would even compete for the love of their children, who in turn were in constant competition with each other.

'"Hudlewrink was able to change this basic animal survival instinct into an intelligent paradigm of empowerment. An empowered neighbour is far more useful to far more people than an exploited one.

'"This shift from exploitation to empowerment was the key to our civilization's eventual unity and advancement. It made our society more cohesive and more powerful. Suddenly there was enough for everyone. We could advance together and realise the mighty potential latent in every individual. We were able to go beyond the petty ignorance that ruled the past, into new areas of amazing advances in personal development and community awareness. It ushered in a peaceful cooperative revolution achieved on top of the dried blood of centuries of bitter competition, conflict and separatism.

'"This shift was achieved by the reclassification of greed and selfishness as a psychological disorder. No longer were greedy, selfish individuals rewarded and admired for their anti-social aberrations. They were hospitalised and treated. Greed and selfishness disorder was easy to diagnose, especially amongst children and once our scientists began to work on the problem it didn't take long to devise a cure.

"'When the greedy, selfish minority were removed from society, it didn't take long for the normally compassionate, hard working masses to reclaim their world from the toxic clutches of the exploiters. For centuries psychopaths had been able to control resources vital to survival, for their own petty aggrandisement. Our history before unification was a disgraceful parade of ego-maniacs battling for the rights to suppress and exploit the innocent masses. They had wrested control of the financial system, all forms of media and entertainment and most horrifying of all they'd wrested control of the food supply. They controlled transport networks and hospitals, weapons and governments. They were able to subvert the destinies of entire nations to fulfill their selfish, generally foolish desires.

"'One of the worst things they collectively foisted upon the other normal members of their species was the suppression of vital discoveries which didn't suit their personal agendas. They were able to strangle society's progress in many areas, especially medical research and food technology. Had we been able to rid ourselves of their pernicious influence a few centuries earlier, we would have advanced far more quickly and a lot of unnecessary suffering and bloodshed could have been avoided.

"'To give one example of the crass, self-serving madness, the helpless peoples of Oc Thit Lip were forced to endure for millennia before unification, I will describe what just one of these megalomaniacs was able to achieve. Six hundred years before unification, a certain trillionaire mounted his company's logo across the surface of the moon. It took four weeks for the monstrosity to be completely installed and then everybody on the home planet could see it. The design itself was rather ingenious. The logo consisted of four colours that appeared in a preordained sequence corresponding with the phases of the moon. The new moon displayed the company's name in a reasonably tasteful shade of pastel pink. Then as the moon entered its next phase, light blue was added and then lavender. Unfortunately the trillionaire had designed the logo himself and was colour-blind. When the moon was full a garish shade of bright green was added. This replicated perfectly the original logo which market research had revealed gave people with normal vision a headache. It was so aesthetically offensive, most people wouldn't look at it and a subsequent survey revealed it was the least recognised logo on the planet. When it suddenly appeared across the surface of the moon, simply ignoring it didn't work anymore. People were forced to look at it in all its tasteless disgustingness. The abomination spewed its ugliness down upon the human race until the trillionaire responsible eventually died and the company was taken over by somebody with normal vision. His first act was to have the company logo redesigned and removed from the moon's surface which still bears the scars from its installation.

"'Initially, the greedy and selfish refused to accept they were a problem. They considered themselves to be gifted paragons of the human condition, a superior elite. They considered the notion that they had a psychological disorder to be laughable. To them it was the common masses who had the problem, being weak and lacking in vision and ambition.

"'Removing them from their positions of power and confiscating their considerable assets was not easy. It required a lot of blood and sacrifice. They weren't prepared to acquiesce without causing as much destruction as they were capable of unleashing upon the armies of reform which stood against them.

"'It was Hudlewrink who inspired this final revolution and reclaimed the destiny of the masses from the centuries old curse of economic slavery which had limited the evolution of society to the sick, selfish whims of the ruthless few. Eventually the forces of greed and selfishness were defeated and the perpetrators incarcerated and forced into treatment and rehabilitation. Some responded favorably and were able to genuinely repent and be reintegrated into society. Most were beyond treatment and remained steadfastly selfish until the end.

"'By reclaiming the resources that are the natural birthright of all humanity, our civilisation was finally able to develop peacefully and productively. Removing the systems based on exploitation and replacing them with systems of empowerment was easy, once the exploiters were gone. Liberation from greed and selfishness led to a period of peace and achievement that lasted nearly 12,000 years. It heralded a golden age of enlightenment and plenty.

"'During this time we explored the other eleven planets in our Star Family and built colonies on most of them. We found intelligent life on one other planet and established friendly relations with them. They are a marine species and were able to survive in our oceans. They set up an embassy in the ocean off the coast near our centre of government and have colonized our oceans to the great benefit of our native marine species. Their home planet has already been completely obliterated by the barrage of meteorites we are attempting to endure as I speak.

"'We sent out probes into deep space and learnt many astonishing secrets about the way the universe is ordered. We were able to find the remaining traces of the mighty race that had engineered humanity in a last desperate, doomed attempt to save themselves from destruction.

"'By the year 10,000 we were beginning to exhaust the supply of Necrolium, our most basic power source, something we'd always just dug from the ground. It consisted of the preserved bodies of a number of species that made the evolutionary leap from cactus to lizard several billion years ago. These species ruled the planet for millions of years until they were superseded by higher life forms. Their bodies didn't decompose like those of mammals, birds or even modern day reptiles. They remained intact and proved to be extremely combustible when combined with seaweed. We burned this to fuel our civilisation but like all finite resources it began to run out.

"'Fortunately our civilisation had advanced beyond the need for such a primitive power source. We learned to harness the subtle energies of the planet and used the last Necrolium to build the planetary power grid, described in the other half of this time capsule.

"'In the year 10,219 the pyramid network was completed.

"'However this did not entirely rid us of all our problems. In the year 11,110 we suffered a terrible calamity. It became known as the Ifab Disaster. Across the planet a new communications system called Ifab was set up to enable anyone to contact anyone else almost instantly using a small headset. We'd used this sort of technology before but in their enthusiasm to improve the lives of their fellow citizens, the developers of Ifab failed to properly test the new technology.

"'After about 200 days using the system, people began to lose consciousness. Then, completely unconscious they crawled to the base of the nearest transmitter and died. The bodies kept piling up in the affected cities for days. It took nearly three weeks to determine the cause and completely shut the system down by which time nearly 70,000 of the largest cities across the face of Oc Thit Lip had most of their population lying dead at the crowded base of an Ifab communications tower. Over 12 billion people died during the six weeks of the tragedy. The worst affected cities had to be abandoned and were sealed beneath domes of adjabraz.' Sorry but we couldn't translate that particular word," explained Hu Ya before returning to the commentary.

"'It took nearly 100 years before the population restabilised after the Ifab Disaster.

"'During this time religious practice was revived. Charismatic leaders emerged who were able to convince many to become followers and believe in an entity that was credited with the creation of time and space. Temples were built and the entity was worshipped openly by the faithful.

"'Our civilisation was severely shaken when a group of wise men from the rebel province of Southern Aldrikes, proved conclusively that such a being could not possibly exist nor could it ever have existed. It was proved to be an anomaly, compounded by superstitious tendencies inflamed by the grief of lost loved ones and a psychological tendency towards dependence due to immaturity.

"'This revelation resulted in the sacking of the priesthood, causing temple doors to be slammed shut and never opened again.

"'The debunking of the Church of Infinite Spirit took place in the year 15,217 and though it seriously undermined the foundations of civilization on Oc Thit Lip, it was not enough to destroy us.

"'During this period a woman rose from the ranks of the ordinary to lead us through another extraordinary period of our history. Her name was Malalajag.

"'Before she became Regent, Malalajag raised seven children on a farm and was famous for her ability to ride horses. Oc Thit Lip thrived under her Regency achieving many great breakthroughs in scientific achievement.

"'One of the most notable discoveries during this period was the final synthesis of our strongest painkillers, our best medicines and our finest motivational potions into the DNA of specifically engineered plants. This fantastic breakthrough enabled us to eliminate most of the side effects caused by the chemicals we'd previously used to treat disease. We devised a process that enabled us to graft our best treatments onto the DNA of certain plants.'"

At this point Hu Ya stopped reading from the translation.

"The botany department was able to identify most of the plants he mentions. The first one was the opium poppy. This is what he said about it. 'This is to stop pain. It can be used effectively as a general anesthetic and can treat all forms of physical, emotional and mental pain. Its greatest application is for treating the dying. Not only does it stop pain, it relieves anxiety and the fear of death.' Next he produced a coca bush, the natural ingredient we use to make cocaine," said Hu Ya before returning to the translation.

"'This is a powerful local anesthetic and can be used to induce short term bursts of energy in emergencies.' Next he showed a peyote cactus," said Hu Ya before once again returning to the translation.

"'This was designed to heighten perception and reset fundamental attitudes. It allowed ordinary people to perceive natural, subtle energies that are otherwise beyond the range of the human senses. It is also very useful in space exploration, increasing the natural range of human perception and physical strength. This enabled us to discover a lot more in alien environments beyond the normal range of our human senses.

"'These were synthesized to cure cluster headaches and to entertain space travelers on long journeys to the outer edges of our Star Family.' At this point he showed some psilocybin mushrooms," Hu Ya interjected into the commentary.

"The commentary continues, 'I am not a therapist so you'll have to excuse me for not being more specific about all these amazing miracle cures.

"'The pinnacle of this technology was the synthesis of the treatment for greed and selfishness disorder into this specially engineered plant.' This is what we refer to as Indian hemp or marijuana," embellished Hu Ya.

"He goes on to claim," Hu Ya continued. "'This plant was the greatest achievement of this particular technology. As well as its curative functions this plant was synthesized to produce a fibre that is superior to anything natural and can be used for making clothing, rope and a host of other extremely useful commodities.

"'These synthesised plants are part of the legacy we proudly leave for future generations. We recommend they be eaten for their latent curative powers to be best utilized. We advise against burning them and inhaling the resultant smoke or injecting them directly into the blood. This is likely to produce some of the harmful side effects these plants were created to avoid. They should not be broken down into their components which were very specifically combined to produce optimal results. Nor should they be used together in multiples. They are very powerful remedies and combinations can produce harmful and unpredictable results.

"'In the year 30,000 Oc Thit Lip had a population of 42 billion with a further 1.4 million people living on colonies in space. The concept of war was left a comfortable distance behind in our history books. Most Oc Thit Lippians were able to lead a comfortable, prosperous, peaceful life.

"'Then came the decadent years. Huge amounts of resources were wasted on meaningless things. Vast edifices constructed for empty, shallow causes. Improbability ruled. A classic example of this was a phobia that was created in the media concerning people with hair on the backs of their hands. Tests were produced that showed a link between most forms of aberrant behavior and excessive hair on the backs of the perpetrator's hands. Mental illness, greed and selfishness were also linked to hairy handed individuals. Villains in children's books were given hairy hands, as were most of the villains in our history.

"'New products were created to remove these unwanted hairs from the backs of unfortunate people's hands. An entire beauty industry based on hand hair removal sprang up.

"'The truly odd thing was that removal of hair from people's hands did actually coincide with a dramatic drop in diagnoses of greed and selfishness.

"'Otherwise during this period, space exploration completely stagnated. We'd pretty much explored our immediate Star Family and were unable to devise a technology that allowed us to cross the enormous distances that separate us from other Star Families.

"'However, technologies evolved that enabled virtual space travel to an unlimited number of destinations without any of the risk and inconvenience associated with actual space travel. As these emerged people lost interest in leaving Oc Thit Lip. It was simpler and more entertaining to create synthetic environments in the comfort of our own homes.

"'By the year 35,000 the population had swelled to 58 billion.

"'Several colonies on Moon seven of the planet Gwentable were damaged by a meteor shower in the year 39,744. This resulted in the deaths of 2117 colonists. It was the worst disaster ever suffered in space before the current catastrophic bombardments began. This further discouraged people from leaving the home planet.

"'In the year 46,279 another major disaster decimated our population. We had become so absorbed in our virtual technologies, the media and our fantasies, we forgot what reality was. The grand edifices we created to amuse ourselves had taken over our lives. We forgot that there's more to life than being entertained.

"'The first event that should have warned us that the road ahead would lead to oblivion was the invention of virtual food. Millions of people starved to death, completely absorbed by the illusion that they were able to survive by consuming what their games provided as sustenance.

"'Then came the invention of the Mindchip. This charming little distraction was actually inserted into the brain so no external devices were needed for people to live permanently inside computer generated holograms.

"'The Mindchip became reality. Once your mind had turned it on you merely had to think of anything and it was in front of you or you were in it. You had instant communication with anybody else, provided they were turned on and wanted to communicate with you. You could be absolutely anywhere, doing anything with any other non body.

"'Then on a fateful afternoon in the year 47,126, update 77197 was installed. It was supposed to add an extra four levels of challenges to give a more competitive edge to athletes competing in ultra-mind sport.

"'What it actually did was to deactivate the entire body of its host from the neck down. Individual Mindchips concluded that only the human head was necessary for its functioning and simply turned the rest of the body off by deactivating all the parts of the brain that controlled everything it considered unnecessary.

"'Mindchip had distracted humanity safely for 157 years. Then over a period of less than two weeks it killed 67% of the population of Oc Thit Lip.

"'Now, we are approaching the end of the year 51,721. Not a particularly remarkable looking number, and yet this number marks the end in solar years of our civilization from the date of Unification.

"'We failed!

"'All our remarkable achievements are about to be swept into the dustbin of oblivion. A giant comet is approaching the inner Star Family and we can only guess at the destruction it will cause.

"'The Planet Mardek has been totally obliterated by a collision with an enormous meteorite roughly a quarter of its mass. The effect on Argeya, the planet between us and what was once Mardek was also catastrophic. It's entire atmosphere was ripped away destroying every living thing on a planet teeming with life.

"'Oc Thit Lip suffered cataclysmic damage when the blast wave hit, tilting the planet's axis by almost two degrees. This destabilised the electro-magnetic field harnessed by the pyramid network and has severely limited the network's effectiveness.

"'By thwarting the natural changes that are the only constant in the universe, we violated the Law of Reciprocal Harmonics. Reality is a result of movement and space. Any interference with the natural processes of movement defies the immutable Law of Change. Greed and selfishness attempt to thwart the process of change by imposing the concept of deferred consumption. The universe has no interest in concepts and will not tolerate stagnation. The pressure builds until finally, inevitably something must break. It appears the cosmos has turned against us.

"'The two great outer Planets, Chreznuff and Demptwix have also been completely destroyed. The effect on our entire Star Family has been profound. We were able to solve the problem of greed and selfishness on an individual and national level but we failed to realise that by setting up our pyramid network and effectively drawing more energy and time from our Star Family, we have been greedy and selfish on a planetary level. The laws of the universe apply equally to individuals as they do to planetary bodies, galaxies and universes. In the same way that the family of a greedy selfish person suffers for the behavior of the exploiter, so it is with a Star Family. It is our planetary brothers and sisters who have so far suffered the worst consequences of our ill considered activities. We built a planetary defense system, capable of destroying or deflecting any incoming stellar bodies away from collision with our home planet. However, this system has already been deployed in its entirety and is the reason why the home planet has so far been able to survive the ravages of bombardment from deep space. The cosmos is not only punishing us but also our entire Star Family.

"'We were able to stabilise and preserve our way of life for almost two Great Years (the time it takes our Star Family to complete a full orbit of the galactic center, 25,920 of our planetary years). We prolonged the life of our civilisation well beyond its natural cycle. We became stagnant, denying the change that is a natural constant of the universe. We dammed the flow of cosmic energy for our selfish purposes attempting to immortalise our civilisation. By drawing more than our naturally allotted share of time and energy, we stopped our spiritual evolution and have brought on horrific destruction to ourselves and our brother and sister planets.

"'If there is a future and if anybody or anything ever sees this, please understand; our failure was our own, nobody else can be blamed.

"'At first the problem we created was small. It was just one of many issues that our Central Council had to deal with. But because of its complexity, they failed to acknowledge its potential and did not deal with it during the time when we might have been saved. As the problem grew, we focused on other, more manageable problems to avoid having to deal with what we had created. Our society was more interested in unreality than reality. The people were distracted by many issues and the truth was ignored for too many years.

"'By the time we couldn't ignore it any more, it was too late.

"'We attempted to expand the network of pyramids onto the other planets in our Star Family, hoping we could stabilise the entire system as we'd stabilised our home planet. We managed to construct seven pyramids on Wojung, the nearest planet to our solar deity. Construction was also begun on our nearest sister Emsra and on our nearest brother Argeya.'"

Again Hu Ya stopped reading from the commentary and explained, "Wojung was their name for Mercury. Emsra, we call Venus and Argeya is most likely Mars," before returning to reading the translation.

"'Then our great scholars decreed that this network, if completed would merely delay the coming reckoning which could potentially destroy our entire galaxy. Construction was halted after the Central Council determined that these measures were nothing more than an attempt to be greedy and selfish, but on a far vaster scale.

"'At this exact moment it appears most likely the approaching comet will pass between Wojung and Emsra. We have no way of predicting the final outcome. Both of these planets host a variety of less evolved life forms.

"'So here am I, recording a history that nobody will probably ever hear. Hey, imaginary nobody, I'm dead! My children are dead. You don't even exist. I'm only doing this because there's nothing else to be done. I spent my whole life studying history; the history of a civilisation that failed; a civilisation that failed to grasp the big picture and the consequences of trying to outsmart the universe. We have no future. The glorious past is now a burden. Our gifted, exceptional ancestors worked heroically for nothing. Their legacies die here. Their great, great, great grand children will die because the time and energy we unwittingly borrowed must be repaid in full.

"'We failed!'"

A long silence followed. The clock ticked noisily and occasional irrelevant noises infiltrated from outside the room. Professor Xu lit a cigarette.

FIFTEEN - THREE SWIRLING YELLOW BAIT FISH

Phuoc laughed. He wasn't very good at laughing and everyone else in the room cringed. Some of them considered running for their lives but decided they were probably safer keeping still and blending into the crowd.

Phuoc looked around the room. He could smell fear, the stench of weakness. He was used to fear but weakness always revolted him.

Phuoc ordered rice wine and moved to a seat where he could see all the cringing, terrified inhabitants of the bar. He savoured the fear as he waited.

He'd spent the previous day becoming an employer. He needed spies. It wasn't for any benevolent reason he chose homeless people. They were abundant, cheap and not likely to be socially connected to Ping or any of her student friends.

Phuoc had a unique system of staff recruitment. It involved finding a comfortable perch near the entrance to a market, proximate to the premises he intended to observe.

His enterprise was blessed by the convenient location of just such a market at the end of Ping's street. He positioned himself in an obvious location near the market's entrance and produced a 20 Yuan note. As always, he held the money out in front of him, as if awaiting the arrival of a recipient. He seldom had to wait more than a few minutes. On this occasion it took only two and a half minutes until a first hopeless, homeless beggar approached him and lunged for the note.

Phuoc allowed the man, roughly his own age, to snatch the note but instantly captured his retreating appendage in the lightning steel grip of his other hand. Unlike most homeless vagrants, the man didn't drop the note. It usually took Phuoc up to 15 or 20 vagrants to find one who didn't instantly drop the note when his thieving hand was accosted.

This one held his stare. Phuoc released his grip.

"I need somebody to watch a house," said Phuoc. "If you can tell me who comes and goes for eight hours, I will give you another 100 Yuan. Do you want to play?"

"Play with yourself!" came the ill-considered reply. Phuoc showed the man several of his yellow, unhealthy teeth. The gesture was enough to repel the man back into the crowd, after Phuoc had reclaimed his investment.

But within 45 minutes Phuoc had three recruits. They weren't particularly impressive specimens. However, they were tenacious, desperate and greedy. One hundred Yuan for an eight hour shift was good money.

The opportunity to sleep in one of the up market, well maintained doorways in Ping's neighbourhood was almost inducement enough. Noticing the arrivals and departures at a specific door was a welcome distraction from the hours of drudgery which was the lot of the homeless.

During his third sip of rice wine the first spy arrived and made his way to Phuoc's table.

"No sign of him," he reported. "I saw the boyfriend arrive just after 9 am and he left just before dark."

"What about the girl?"

"I didn't see her."

Phuoc grunted irritably and took another sip.

"Go back tomorrow and I'll see you here at the same time." He handed the grateful man a 100 Yuan note.

"Thank you. I'll see you tomorrow."

An hour later Phuoc was finishing his wine when another man joined him at his table.

"I didn't see anybody all night," he reported.

"Go back and watch again tonight," grunted Phuoc, handing another note under the table.

The man nodded and left.

Phuoc looked belligerently around the bar. The other patrons had strategically relocated to environments less intimidating and the barman busied himself polishing glasses. Phuoc paid him and left.

Outside it was getting dark. Phuoc made his way back to his other new hotel on the other side of the university campus, well away from the bloodied remains of his last female employee.

The next afternoon he returned to the bar. His first spy was waiting for him.

"The boyfriend arrived just before 9 am and he and the girl both left at 10 am," he reported eagerly. "When I left to come here at 3 pm, neither had returned."

Phuoc handed him a 100 Yuan note and smiled faintly. He rose from his table and accompanied his spy to the door, pausing briefly to pay the barman. Once outside Phuoc turned left and the spy turned right.

* * *

Nearby, inside a tutorial room, the excitement was so intense it was causing Professor Xu to experience heart palpitations. He sat next to Professor Guo, who was almost laughing as he instructed Hu Ya to read from the transcript he was holding.

Ping gripped Tashi's hand tightly as Hu Ya spoke.

"We now have a translation of the final piece," he announced excitedly. "There are a lot of technical terms but the more we translate, the more we are learning their language. What I'm going to read is amazing but please understand that we don't have words for some of what they are trying to tell us and have filled in the gaps as best we could. Ok." He took a deep breath.

"'People of the future, we send you our love. We hope you receive our love in the spirit that it is sent to you. Our civilisation is proud to bless you with our finest achievement. If you have been able to understand our message then you will be able to appreciate our gift to you, the children of our children's children.

"'For many thousands of years our greatest minds worked tirelessly to unravel the mystery of ultimate empowerment. At first we relied on explosion/combustion technologies to power our civilisation. This transitional phase enabled us to advance towards the ultimate freedom of harnessing the natural energies generated by the rotation of the planet itself. Oc Thit Lip', from now on I will use the word Earth whenever they refer to our planet," said Hu Ya before returning to the commentary.

"'Earth is a giant cosmic generator, as are all rotating spherical bodies. The Earth is surrounded by a natural electromagnetic field with specific lines of energy that enfold its surface.'" Once again Hu Ya interrupted the commentary he was reading.

"At this point the whale song was very precise and we were able to translate the ancient language very clearly into whale. However, though we could translate from the whale song, the following section appears to have made far more sense to the whales, possibly because they use these electromagnetic energy lines for navigation. The transcript goes into great detail about something called 'the electromagnetic 1746 planetary grid,' which appears to be a component of, and once again I'm quoting directly from the translated whale song, 'our Star Family's poly-hedronic crystal grid'. There followed quite a lot of detail and we were able to translate what seemed to be some mathematical equations but we have nothing to relate them to in terms of contemporary human understanding."

"The translation went on to state: 'At the places where these lines of energy cross we discovered a source of energy which we were able to concentrate and utilise to power all our technology. At certain key points around this planetary grid we built free energy accelerators and were able to broadcast this energy in a form which could be used anywhere on the planet's surface. At the center of this network we created the dominant controlling structure.'

"Our language is either inadequate to convey these concepts accurately or the translation failed to reveal precisely what they were attempting to express," Hu Ya interjected into the commentary. "So please understand these limitations while I continue with the transcript."

Professor Xu held a burnt out cigarette butt and looked like he was trying to use his mouth to catch flies. Professor Guo smiled happily. Tashi felt like he was watching a highly improbable science fiction movie while Ping just stared at Hu Ya in amazement.

Hu Ya took another deep breath and continued.

"'The structures are four sided pyramids,' we had to insert this term into the translation," explained Hu Ya. "It was the nearest word that corresponded to the description that follows.

"'We designed and built a network of 62 pyramids, created to enhance energy and consciousness using the natural electromagnetic planetary grid and sound. Each pyramid has four triangular sides which generate a specific beneficial energy. The energies are concentrated at the apex of each pyramid and broadcast across the entire surface of the planet.

"'They were built using sonic levitation techniques, a basic technology any civilisation capable of activating this time capsule will, no doubt, be aware of.

"'The entire network is designed to capture and amplify the natural energy that exists abundantly in the Earth's atmosphere and is reinvigorated every day by the sun as its heat and light interact with the natural electro-magnetic force field surrounding the planet as it rotates. This energy produces no pollution, or any other type of disturbance to life or any of the planet's natural systems.'

"At this point a map appeared that according to the transcript shows the locations of all the parts of the planetary pyramid network," interjected Hu Ya. "The map also shows the locations of the cities that were sealed tombs after the Ifab disaster that Rupkey described in the previous revelation."

Professor Guo turned on a projector which cast an image onto a screen showing the surface of a planet which bore little resemblance to the Earth they now inhabited. It had several land masses and vast areas of ocean but nothing was immediately recognisable in modern geographic depiction. It showed the network of pyramids as a series of purple triangles and there were large areas that were coloured grey. The sphere emulated the rotation of the planet and revealed a uniform pattern of purple triangles with one larger golden triangle and a series of red lines that connected them together with a separate series of green lines that connected all the purple triangles to the large golden one.

"We think the grey areas indicate the cities that were buried following what the previous revelation referred to as the Ifab disaster," explained Professor Guo.

"There's more," continued Hu Ya.

"'The base of the central pyramid has four sides which were created to produce four distinct energy/consciousness fields. The first of these is an energy source which can be harnessed by any technology constructed within similar parameters to the artefact that contains this message. The fact that you are able to activate this time capsule and retrieve this information means that you are technically advanced enough to be able to construct similar devices which can be similarly activated to perform whatever functions you require of them. This is a free energy accelerator, converting the Earth's natural electromagnetic field into a power source that can be used anywhere on the planet.

"'Once the network was in place and was radiating natural energy, we were able to activate the second side of the base, the first of two consciousness accelerators to radiate enlightenment.'

"At this point modern language failed us and what follows is at best a guess at what the ancients were attempting to convey. Some of the terms are translatable but the basic concepts have very little that we can relate them to, outside certain terminologies used by some of the world's religions. The program we used was easily able to translate these ideas into communicable whale song. However modern human language simply doesn't deal with ideas like these. They appear to be referring to some sort of process of spiritual uplifting, some kind of mental meditative tranquility that somehow pacified or calmed negative emotional states of mind."

He looked over the stunned gathering hoping somebody might have some opinion to help qualify what he had attempted to say. His gaze was met with stupefied wonder from all except Tashi, who shook his head dumbly in a state beyond mystification. Hu Ya inhaled and continued.

"'Attached to the central pyramid was a group or clan of what seem to be described as highly realised adepts. Their mind energies or perhaps meditations were somehow transmitted across the network, apparently uniting some fundamental psychic force that projected peace or serenity or some type of inherent dignity or perhaps ennoblement into the soul consciousness of all living beings, even including the animals and plants.'

"That was the end of what we could even vaguely understand about this function," explained Hu Ya. "There were another seven minutes of dialogue that was probably devoted to embellishing these ideas, but as yet we haven't been able to make any sense of it whatsoever. All we could discern was something about balancing the sacred feminine with the sacred masculine and a very esoteric description of how this was achieved. It all seemed to make perfect sense in whale song and hopefully as we understand more of it we should be able to translate more into human language.

"The third side of the base of the central pyramid appears to relate to the geology or perhaps geography of the Earth," Hu Ya attempted to explain. "It was described as 'the second energy component'. The commentary states;

"'The pyramid network was also used to stabilise the Earth's electromagnetic field and enabled us to prevent natural disasters, including earthquakes, volcanic eruptions and violent meteorological events like hurricanes and severe droughts. We were able to halt the natural cycle of cataclysms that otherwise occur every 5,200 years and were responsible for the destruction of most of the previous civilisations that had arisen prior to our own. This enabled us to progress further than any previous civilisation, the ruins of which can be located across most of the planet's land masses. It allowed our culture to survive for nearly two Great Years and prevented the natural electromagnetic shifts that proved so disastrous in the past.'

"The fourth and final side of the central pyramid's base was described as the second consciousness aspect," explained Hu Ya before returning to the translation.

"'It infused the astral plane with wisdom. This manifested in every individual as an intuition that placed the ancient truths of our greatest philosophers at everybody's disposal. It ended ignorance and superstition even amongst the most isolated populations. It put an end to barbaric practices and many types of foolishness which had previously limited our evolution. The result was a population grounded in ethics and justice.

"'Finally, all the pyramids were designed to promote physical health and longevity through the healing power of sound. Inside each pyramid is either one, two or in the case of the central pyramid, three chambers with a resonant frequency that will aid and augment the natural life forces of the physical bodies living within its sphere of influence. They each sound a different note or combination of notes according to their location and the requirements of healthy bodies according to the climate and various other local variables. Each pyramid sounds its note at dawn as the sun activates it and the electromagnetic field it draws its power from. The effect of each pyramid sounding its note or notes as the planet rotates produces a melody that resonates with all living creatures.

"'The melody required to activate this time capsule in its entirety is the same as the melody produced by the network of pyramids. The melody required to activate the other half dealing with our civilisation's history, stimulates the heart, the circulation system and the four lower chakras, while the melody required to activate this half stimulates the brain, the endocrine system and the three higher chakras. Everyone who has witnessed the activation of the whole and its parts will notice an immediate improvement in their physical well being, increased energy levels and greater dexterity and strength.'"

Hu Ya paused. He'd read the entire transcript twice before, once when it was first printed out and a second time with Professor Guo. Its impact wasn't mitigated by having read it before and he could see his audience was exhausted by what they were attempting to absorb.

"It comes with a warning," he said. Everyone emitted a sigh, almost of relief as if the overwhelming positivity they'd just heard needed something less than wonderful to place it into their shattered reality.

"'The apex of the pyramids must never be capped. If they cannot dissipate the energies within them, they will explode. The explosion will, at the very least, damage the pyramid itself and could possibly, depending on the amount of energy trapped, cause considerable damage to the surrounding area.'"

"That could explain why the Archeology building burnt down," interjected Professor Guo excitedly.

"What has the Archeology building got to do with a network of ancient pyramids?" asked Professor Xu attempting to find another cigarette.

"Because we partially activated the Oracle but it wasn't able to fully discharge the energy it had absorbed and then we effectively capped it by locking it in the safe," replied Professor Guo triumphantly.

"That is a reasonably plausible theory, I suppose," conceded Professor Xu, producing his lighter.

"It's a lot more plausible than any of the other explanations," replied Professor Guo.

"What other explanations?" asked Ping.

"Exactly," surmised Professor Guo. "Nobody has been able to come up with any other explanation. Continue please, Hu Ya."

"The revelation ended with the following, and I would like to stress once again that a lot of this is guess work, based on what were considered the most likely meanings of the words in their context.

"'To access this, our greatest legacy, first you must confirm that the master pyramid, or Pyramid Asia, or possibly three swirling yellow bait fish, is still active and functioning. It is the key, the central control which will allow you to empower your world. It is situated at the centre of the grid and its formidable structure should be easy to locate provided it has survived intact. All the pyramids were constructed from stone and were designed to last for hundreds of thousands of years. The master pyramid is clearly marked in gold on the map we have provided. Even if some of the other parts of the network have been damaged or destroyed, the centre will still generate the energies described above and should be used for the benefit of all life.

"'We bequeath this to you with our blessing and our fervent desire that your civilisation will be able to use it to surpass our achievements. May you rise to glorious heights and usher in another golden age of life on our beloved Earth. We wish peace, love and enlightenment to all who are able to hear our message.'"

SIXTEEN - FORCED ENTRY

Phuoc made his way to Ping's flat. He had a small crowbar in his pocket and was very adept at using it to force entry into places where he wasn't welcome. He intended to break in, now that his spies all assured him Ping and Tashi weren't there. If Irfan was hiding inside he would find him and complete his assignment. If not he would search the flat for clues and plant the bug Dan Ban Ho had given him.

He rounded the last corner and immediately stopped. A small group of people were hovering in front of Ping's door. Some of them had cameras. He guessed they must be news reporters as he turned and strode briskly back the way he'd come, hoping none of them had seen him.

The blind rage, never far from his waking thoughts and starring in his dreams, rushed up his spine and reclaimed its throne in his frontal cortex. Why hadn't his spies told him the place was being staked out? He hurried back to the hotel.

Perhaps the violence and arrest in the park had provoked the attention of the media.

Fortunately for them, nobody noticed him slip through the entrance of the ramshackle dump which had grudgingly accepted his patronage. He climbed the rickety stairs to unlock the dilapidated door to his room. With it locked safely behind him he fell into a chair which, along with the vermin infested, old, hard bed, comprised the sum total of the room's furnishings. He unscrewed the top of a half empty bottle of rice wine sitting within range on the dirty wooden floor.

* * *

Back at the university, Hu Ya had concluded his presentation. He sat down aware that he'd shorted out everyone in the room's rational mental circuitry. Tashi was the first to re-contact the self he had been before Hu Ya's improbable deluge forever re-landscaped his mental geography.

"That's not possible," he whispered.

That was enough to drag the rest of the gathering back into present time. Professor Xu coughed loudly. Professor Guo beamed silently and shook his head, more to make sure it was still there than as a form of disagreement. Ping started to cry.

Hu Ya tried to mumble something about it not being 100% certain and other translations were possible.

"Can we see the map again?" asked Professor Xu trying valiantly to re-establish some sort of academic framework. Anything concrete his intellect could deal with would suffice, while he attempted to reign in his highly unprofessional, rioting emotions by smoking yet another cigarette.

Professor Guo turned on the projector and the alien map reappeared on the screen.

"Can anybody recognize anything?" gasped Professor Xu.

"Can we assume the top is north and the bottom south?" answered Hu Ya.

"Why?"asked Professor Xu.

"I can invert it," offered Professor Guo.

The resultant image was no more recognizable than a stain on a table cloth.

"That places a land mass on the bottom which could be the Antarctic," offered Professor Xu mustering his otherwise completely eclipsed analytical powers.

"Good point," agreed Professor Guo. "The large island above it could be Australia," he added.

"Yes, but that would place the larger land mass to its right in the middle of what is now the Pacific Ocean," interjected Tashi.

"The legendary continent of Lumeria, perhaps," suggested Professor Xu.

"What about Atlantis?" asked Ping who'd recovered sufficiently to form words.

"Atlantis is a myth," said Tashi dismissively.

"So is Lumeria," replied Professor Xu.

As the globe rotated, Professor Guo exclaimed excitedly, "There's America and Atlantis and that must be an early version of Africa."

"So where's Europe?" asked Tashi.

"Under water. The next big landmass with the golden pyramid in the middle, is probably early Asia," stated Professor Xu, igniting another cigarette.

"You people are crazy!" said Tashi. "That was the biggest fairy tale I've ever heard in my life. How can you take any of this seriously?"

There was an enormous emotional release as everyone burst out laughing.

"You think this is some kind of hoax?" asked Professor Xu, after a few hearty puffs. "Do you think somebody created this artefact and all of this is fake? We don't have the technology to do what we've all seen. Even if the information is nonsense, the technology required to produce it is beyond anything we have today."

There was a knock on the door. Ping almost jumped off her chair.

Professor Guo looked apologetically around the room and shrugged his shoulders. Whatever was happening outside the tutorial room was so inconsequential by comparison, it barely rated as a distraction.

A further, somewhat more insistent knock followed and the door opened slightly to reveal Professor Guo's secretary peering into the room. Without making an entrance, she apologetically exclaimed, "I'm very sorry to interrupt but we have a rather large contingent of media insisting they speak with you. I've managed to keep them contained in the outer lecture complex but they are becoming increasingly more insistent. They are demanding to speak to you."

"Media?" Professor Guo spat the word out as if a fly had flown into his mouth.

"They're mainly from CCTV and there are also some local newspaper journalists as well."

"What do they want?" demanded Professor Xu.

"They want to speak with the Head of the Archeology Department."

"Did they say what they want to talk to me about?" asked Professor Guo suddenly faced with the reality of the fame he had tentatively considered might be coming his way.

"They say they've received information from one of the cameramen who filmed some event involving you at the Party Secretary's house last week."

"Let me handle this," said Professor Xu, stubbing out a half smoked butt. "I suggest the rest of you leave via the fire escape. I'll try to distract them. The minibus is in the car park. Tell the driver to take you to the Winter Garden Hotel and I'll meet you there as soon as I can get away."

Nobody argued. Even Tashi was suddenly prepared to accept that the situation was serious and with Ping holding his hand tightly, they all quietly filed out of the room.

* * *

Back in his cupboard, Irfan was terrified. He could hear something happening outside in the street. He wasn't going to open the door under any circumstances. Whoever was there, would have to come in and drag him out. He'd feared that somebody would attempt to get to him as soon as he was alone and had begged Ping not to leave him in the flat.

She and Tashi had been summoned to the university for something special. Tashi said it was important but Irfan failed to understand why they both needed to go. He knew it had something to do with the ornament Dan Ban Ho had already used to try to get to him and suspected the urgent meeting was a set up to get them out of the flat.

He huddled in the dark, praying silently to Allah. He tried to pray facing Mecca but couldn't be sure of the exact direction. He'd managed to make himself reasonably comfortable in the small space by taking down the shelves and stacking them against the wall. This gave him a little more room and meant he could stand up. His bad leg ached at night because he had to sleep curled up on the floor. This didn't bother him. He was grateful to have somewhere to hide, now he knew Dan Ban Ho was looking for him. He had no choice but to trust Allah and so far Allah had kept him alive.

* * *

The hotel was a lot more comfortable than the tutorial room but nobody noticed. While they waited for Professor Xu, Professor Guo produced a copy of the map drawn onto a flat piece of paper and spread it out on a coffee table.

"If we can locate some of these pyramids, we can determine whether or not they still exist and see if they still function," he said enthusiastically.

"If they really are over 300,000 years old, there's not much chance of that," said Tashi, despite having been lectured by Ping all the way from the university to stop being so negative.

"Even if we can find one or two of the sites where they once stood, that will be a remarkable discovery," answered Professor Guo, undeterred by Tashi's insistence that the entire event had been some cleverly crafted illusion.

"If we assume the central pyramid is the Great Pyramid at Giza in Egypt, we might have a starting point," suggested Hu Ya.

"Even I know that the Great Pyramid isn't 300,000 years old," said Tashi.

"What if some other civilisation found the artefact, activated it and attempted to recreate the network?" said Ping determined not to succumb to rational limitations.

"We need a modern atlas," she suggested. "If we could overlay the ancient map onto a modern one then we could see if any of the sites correspond to anything still in existence."

"That's a good idea," agreed Professor Guo.

"I noticed a bookshop on this street when we pulled into the hotel car park," said Tashi.

Professor Guo fumbled in his coat and produced his wallet. "Go and see if they have an atlas," he said giving Hu Ya a crisp 3,000 Yuan note. "This should be enough."

Hu Ya took the money. "Do we need anything else?" he asked.

Tashi refrained from asking for food, even though he was hungry. Nobody else could think of anything that might otherwise be useful.

After another few minutes of what could best be described as random speculation, there was a knock on the door.

"That was quick," said Ping rising to let Hu Ya back in. She opened the door to find Professor Xu.

"I told the media it was a hoax," he explained as he joined the others around the mysterious map. "I don't think they were entirely convinced but hopefully they'll leave us alone for a while. Some of them tried to follow me but I lost them in the back streets."

"How much do they know?" asked Professor Guo.

"One of the cameramen has a brother who works for CCTV in Xi'an. He told his brother what he'd seen. I don't think any of them believed his story so it wasn't hard to get rid of them. But now the story is out, we have to start taking more serious precautions. I think you and Tashi should go into hiding," said Professor Xu to Ping. "The artefact is safely locked away but they'll probably still try to find you. They know Tashi found it and apparently there are some reporters waiting for you outside your house."

"Irfan will be terrified," said Ping.

There was another knock on the door. This time it was Hu Ya with a map of the modern world. The two maps were spread out side by side on the floor.

"Show us where you found the artefact," instructed Professor Xu refraining from lighting another cigarette.

Tashi pointed to Mt Luguna.

"If we assume that to be the central pyramid, let's mark the relative positions of the other pyramids from the original map," suggested Professor Xu.

Professor Guo produced a pencil and after some debate, parts of the network were duplicated onto the modern map.

"That's very interesting," commented Professor Guo. "Some of them appear quite close to some modern sites. This one isn't far from Stonehenge and this one is near the Yucatan Peninsula in Mexico."

"Most of them are in the ocean," noted Tashi.

"Let's try again assuming the Great Pyramids of Egypt are the central pyramid," suggested Hu Ya, a second time.

This placed even more of the ancient network under water.

"There's not much correspondence to anything accept the Great Pyramid itself," noted Professor Guo. "The other map looked better."

"What if we move the pyramids that correspond to Chitchen Itza in the Yucatan and Stonehenge to those sites and see where that places the rest," suggested Ping.

"More of them are on land," noted Tashi.

"That's much better," agreed Professor Xu. "That puts the central pyramid in modern day western Tibet."

"Wow," concurred Hu Ya.

"That places the central pyramid right on top of Mt Kailash," said Professor Guo looking up from the map with an expression of contagious amazement.

Even Tashi was astounded.

"Does anybody know anything about Mt Kailash?" asked Professor Xu fumbling for a cigarette.

"It's not very accessible," answered Professor Guo. "I don't think there's a road that goes near it."

"Let's see where the rest of the network falls if we assume Mt Kailash is the central pyramid," said Professor Xu, eager to discover more.

"This is only a very rough approximation," said Professor Guo.

"There's definitely one at Giza," said Ping.

"These four are in the middle of the Pacific Ocean," commented Tashi.

"Another three are in the Atlantic corresponding to what was probably Atlantis," exclaimed Professor Xu excitedly. "Two in modern Australia and it looks like there were others in North and South America, some more in Africa and even one in Antarctica."

"This one is in China," said Tashi finally joining in the enthusiasm.

"This is amazing," proclaimed Hu Ya.

"We need to take this back to the university and make a proper map out of clear plastic so we can place them all more accurately," said Professor Guo.

"Nobody is to breathe a word of this to anybody," said Professor Xu, wheezing excitedly as he sucked on his cigarette.

"Ping and Tashi, take the minibus. Go home and pack a bag each and find somewhere nice and remote to hide until we can prepare a proper academic paper to present to the world," instructed Professor Xu

"Where should we go?" asked Tashi.

"What about Irfan?" asked Ping.

"Leave him. He doesn't have anything to do with this," wheezed Professor Xu.

"I can't leave him. My father's enemies want to kill him. He's my father's only hope."

"Take him with you if you must," conceded Professor Xu. "But don't tell him about any of this. Don't tell anybody."

"Where shall we go?" repeated Tashi.

"Let's go back to your village," suggested Ping. "We can hide out at your parent's house."

"We won't have to worry about any news reporters there," agreed Tashi.

"As long as we can contact you," said Professor Guo. "We don't want you disappearing off the face of the planet.

SEVENTEEN - STRICTLY FORBIDDEN

Dan Ban Ho paced the floor of his hotel suite. No news was bad news and he preferred being the cause of bad news to being its recipient. Several days had passed and the black Mercedes hadn't returned. He had no idea what had happened to its occupants. They had obviously failed, but the consequences were uncertain. He had seen a news report showing Inspector Ding Cum being arrested, although it was unclear on what charges and whether or not they related to anything involving him or his dealings with the Xian'yang Police Department.

Every member of his organisation possessed a cell phone but all were strictly forbidden to use them to make contact with the organisation, especially in dangerous situations.

This affair had already wasted far too much of his precious time. Normally he wouldn't have bothered to become so personally involved in a simple execution but something about the strange artefact had lured him into more participation than was prudent. Now he regretted his impulsiveness and recognised that he was the sole architect of his own predicament.

It appeared somebody had better contacts than he did. This usually meant that this other person would soon be found lying in a ditch somewhere, having donated most of their major organs to some hungry pigs. Somebody was tampering with Dan Ban Ho's script and he didn't like it.

He managed to keep himself occupied by terrorising the managers and staff of the legitimate business interests he controlled in Xi'an. One of the few shimmers of light relief came from a report that the manager of the Golden Lotus Hotel was considering committing suicide.

Otherwise, he had achieved nothing. Reluctantly, he caught a flight back to Shanghai. If Phuoc was still operational as the rumours suggested, he would know that his continuing status as 'operational' was entirely dependent upon the completion of his assignment.

* * *

Phuoc preferred to work at night. Darkness was one of his few friends. He retraced his footsteps of the previous morning, satisfied his cloak of anonymity was an unholy shield, behind which he was free to commit whatever atrocities he deemed appropriate.

He had fired all his spies that afternoon. They left disgruntled, grumbling and unpaid.

The rabble that curtailed his earlier efforts had dispersed, allowing him unimpeded access to the door which his small crow bar massaged out of the way. Once inside he was surprised to find his old friend, darkness. The silence he expected to be exclusively at his service was doing a double shift in the employ of his target, who wasn't where Phuoc had hoped to find him. Without his intended victim, his entire enterprise hovered impotently in the realm of mere misdemeanor.

He planted the bug.

Thwarted for a second time in one day he returned to his hotel, frustrated and angry.

Meanwhile, in a minibus almost 100 kilometres away, Irfan was attempting to explain in his less than eloquent Tibetan, how Ping's father had been set up by Dan Ban Ho.

"They switched the labels on the containers and forged the consignment documents," he tried to explain.

Tashi understood that something on some ships had been swapped to make some officials nervous. Ping thought he was describing corruption at the port of Hong Kong and besides the implication that her father was somehow involved, she was unable to glean anything. After almost an hour of polite miscomprehension, Ping and Tashi reverted to speaking Mandarin, confident that Irfan would have less chance of understanding them than they had of understanding him.

After leaving the hotel, they had returned to Ping's flat, to find one last dedicated reporter from a local newspaper camped outside the front door. They easily parried his barrage of questions by laughing at him and pretending his allegations were ludicrous. Tashi produced his student ID, showing he was enrolled in the dentistry faculty as Ping unlocked the front door and they disappeared inside, threatening to call the police.

Once inside Irfan was mightily relieved to see them and happy to gather his meager possessions, as soon as he understood they were leaving. He didn't care where they were going. His only desire, dwarfed by his desperation to leave, was that their destination might provide a slightly larger cupboard for him to hide inside.

The lone reporter had accepted the futility of his surveillance by the time Ping had packed a few possessions and they made their way back to the minibus parked discretely in an adjoining street.

The two minute walk was excruciating. Ping and Tashi expected to be accosted by reporters at any moment while Irfan didn't expect to survive. The usual late afternoon chaotic flow of purposeful pedestrians ignored their desperate passage and as soon as they turned the corner, they ran to the sanctuary of the minibus. They threw their bags in and instructed the driver to drive!

They began to relax as the sights and sounds of Xian'yang faded behind them and they were swallowed whole by the accommodatingly anonymous countryside.

Irfan was relieved beyond the boundaries of language to have left the city. After he gave up trying to tell them what he knew about why Ping's father was in jail, he relaxed for the first time in what felt like weeks. The country air in his lungs was a wonderful reward after what he'd been forced to endure. He silently thanked Allah and prayed that his ordeal might soon be over as the other two passengers maintained an excited dialogue beyond the threshold of his comprehension.

As night reclaimed the fields of wheat and corn, Allah granted him peace. Irfan was soon dreaming of mountains and streams fed by melting snow. The birds were singing and his daughter brought him a bunch of flowers she had picked from the valley near their village.

The next morning Irfan woke before dawn. It was cooler than when he had gone to sleep. The minibus was still moving along a peaceful country road. The driver noticed he had awoken and gave him a warm smile. Tashi and Ping were asleep beside him. He began to recite his morning prayers, silently giving thanks to Allah for everything. Gratitude warmed his soul as he watched the first rays of the sun flash playfully between the distant snow covered peaks. He felt privileged to be part of the majestic beauty of creation. He marveled at the serene genius behind such wonder.

The minibus hit a deep pothole and he and the other two passengers were thrown from their seats. Irfan couldn't help himself and laughed as Ping and Tashi were rudely wrenched from their slumber. Almighty Allah had a sense of humor and he felt privileged being the only person who could appreciate the joke.

* * *

Professor Guo was still in his office as the first rays of the sun began to illuminate the university campus. He re-read the transcript Hu Ya had presented the previous afternoon. As he was nearing the end there was a tentative knock on his office door.

Professor Xu didn't wait to be invited in. "Good morning," he muttered. "I couldn't sleep either.".

"We need to make a more accurate map," said Professor Guo.

Professor Xu lit a cigarette.

Half an hour later the two men were ready to overlay a meticulously marked acetate sheet on a map of the modern world.

"The shaded areas correspond with our modern oil fields," noted Professor Xu between puffs. "The large areas cover most of the Middle East, the Gulf of Mexico up through Texas."

"Modern Alaska, and other parts of Africa especially Nigeria and right across the Sahara," added Professor Guo.

"Do you think it's possible that our modern day oil fields are the result of the Ifab disaster?"

"There's definitely a very strong correspondence."

"The geologists aren't going to like this."

"Look at where the pyramids are situated," said Professor Guo. "There's one on nearly every sacred site in the ancient world."

"This is going to rewrite our entire concept of history. Besides a few legends, like Atlantis and Lumeria, we've always assumed our modern civilisation was the peak of human achievement. This is going to consign most of our current academic thinking into a trash can," said Professor Xu happily.

"Entire libraries full of cherished theories are going to be shown to be no more than fanciful, ill-conceived nonsense," added Professor Guo.

"A lot of people aren't going to like this."

For the second time that morning, the door displayed its propensity to be knocked. The two professors looked at each other like a pair of naughty children, then hastily separated the maps and consigned them to a cupboard.

Professor Guo glided towards the threatening portal and after a quick survey of the room, opened the door.

Hu Ya was awaiting him on the other side.

"I'm sorry to interrupt," he began apologetically, acknowledging the presence of Professor Xu with a respectful nod. "I haven't been able to sleep all night and I was wondering if I could help in any way."

"You're not the only one," muttered Professor Xu.

"We've made a more accurate map," said Professor Guo.

"There doesn't seem to be any point trying to hide it from you," conceded Professor Xu opening the cupboard. The two maps were once again spread out across the desk.

"Wow! That's amazing," was all that Hu Ya could add.

"We need to find out more about Mt Kailash," said Professor Xu as the three of them studied the maps in otherwise mesmerised silence.

"That's something useful you can do," said Professor Guo to Hu Ya. "Go to the university library and see what you can find about Mt Kailash."

"And while you're there," added Professor Xu, "see what you can find out about dragon lines or ley lines as they're known in the west."

* * *

Happiness wasn't a word that was ever used in relation to Phuoc. Belligerence and festering evil were. However in his current state, even they failed to come close to describing the orgy of apocalyptic discontent that was brewing somewhere between his furrowed brow and the small pony tail on the back of his head. At the centre of the storm was a cold, still, alter of evil where his reptilic core was calmly attempting to calculate where Irfan could have escaped to.

Irfan wouldn't be the first of Phuoc's intended victims to take his own life. However Phuoc doubted this because the two students had disappeared with him. The three of them had gone somewhere, the only relevant question was where?

And then there were irrelevant questions like what had happened to his boss and the other body guard? Were they dead? Were they in jail? He considered it unlikely that Dan Ban Ho would be back in jail.

That night he dreamt of the rice fields in Vietnam and the deadly sound of approaching helicopters. He awoke several times during the night with the taste of napalm burning his tongue.

The next morning he woke up early, the bed drenched in sweat. On this occasion there were no casualties.

Phuoc had no choice but to contact Dan Ban Ho's office and report his failure. He knew far better than to even contemplate using his cell phone. There was a payphone in the hotel lobby. He inserted some coins, dialed and waited.

In Shanghai, Dan Ban Ho was both relieved and furious. It was bad enough that one of his bodyguards was dead and the other still incarcerated inside a money-proof police cell in Xi'an, but the news that Irfan was not only alive but had disappeared was intolerable.

"Stay where you are, you fool!" he bellowed down the line. "Phone me at the same time tomorrow. I need time to sort out the mess you've made!"

The line went dead in Phuoc's hand. He left the hotel and headed for a bar. Maybe he could find somebody else to kill while he waited.

Now the problem of finding Irfan belonged to Dan Ban Ho. He remained at his desk as a plan formed involving Ping and her mother. If Irfan was with Ping then he would get her mother to find them for him. He didn't imagine they would have gone very far, and then Phuoc could finish the job.

Later that afternoon Dan Ban Ho was shown into the private hospital suite where Ping's mother had been recuperating since the night of her husband's arrest. He was accompanied by Constable Chang of the Hong Kong Police Department, who had met him at the airport and driven them both to the hospital. Constable Chang was grateful for an opportunity to be of service to Dan Ban Ho. After Ho's arrest and subsequent trial, Constable Chang had no doubt that he would have been wearing his police uniform inside a coffin in the Hong Kong cemetery, had Ho been convicted.

They had to wait half an hour for the shot the doctor administered to take effect so that Ping's mother would be aware of what she was about to be told.

They sat patiently next to her bed as she slowly became conscious.

"Who are you?" she finally asked, shocked to find herself able to so easily enunciate the words.

"We're from the Hong Kong Police," replied Ho not even bothering to flash the fake ID he had in his pocket.

"What do you want?"

"We're here to warn you that your daughter is in great danger," said Ho.

"What's happened to Ping?"

"We're not sure. She's disappeared."

"Oh no! Not my darling Ping as well?" She began to sob but then lost interest, having been rendered chemically incapable of one of her usual performances.

"Don't worry," reassured Constable Chang in the finest tradition of the not so common good cop/good cop routine. "If you can tell us where she is, we'll arrange 24 hour protection for her."

"She's gone back to Xian'yang University."

"I'm sorry to have to inform you but she seems to have disappeared from there," purred Ho, straining to stay within the parameters dictating 'good cop' behavior.

"We were hoping you might have some idea where she may have gone," he added with all the charm he could muster.

"I don't know. Unless she went back to her boyfriend's parent's house."

"And where might that be?" chimed Ho sweetly.

"Somewhere in Tibet. They live in a small village near Lhasa."

"Can you remember the name of the village?"

"It was Womadige."

"Thank you so much. You've been very helpful." Dan Ban Ho paused. "Does she have a cell phone?" he asked trying to lace his voice with fatherly concern. "If she's not in Womadige, we still need some way to contact her."

Ping's mother opened a drawer beside her bed and produced her own phone. She fumbled with the buttons on its face for a few seconds before handing it to Dan Ban Ho. He gave it to Constable Chang who produced a regulation police notebook and pen and wrote down the number displayed on the phone's small screen.

"Thank you for your help," purred Ho. "We won't take up any more of your time."

Barely able to suppress the smirk threatening to invade his face, Ho stood up and he and Constable Chang cordially left.

* * *

When Hu Ya finally arrived back from the library he had two books. The two professors had spent most of the intervening time moving the acetate sheet around on top of the modern world map, trying to find alternatives to their initial positioning. No other way of placement was able to link up as many known ancient sacred sites as placing the central pyramid over Mt Kailash.

"What did you find out about Mt Kailash?' asked Professor Guo enthusiastically.

"Not much," was the disappointing reply. "The library contained very little information about Tibet."

"Isn't this supposed to be the Institute of Tibetan Nationalities?" asked an exasperated, over-tired Professor Xu from behind yet another cloud of cigarette smoke.

"We are here to re-educate Tibetans," explained Professor Guo.

"I located it in several atlases but wasn't able to find out much more than what we already have on the map. These two books contain information about dragon lines."

"Let me see them," said Professor Xu taking the books from Hu Ya.

"This one is called 'Geopathic Stress Healing' and the other is 'Rainbow Serpent Dreaming'. What has any of that got to do with dragon lines?" asked Professor Xu unable to conceal his annoyance at what seemed to be becoming a waste of time.

"The first one mentions dragon lines and the effect they can have on people's health," explained Hu Ya. "Here. Read this," he said opening the book and handing it back to Professor Xu.

"'Dragon Lines are the pathways of electromagnetism and life-force that spread like a web across the surface of the planet. Where the dragon's breath is sweet and gentle, great health and prosperity will arise. Where the dragon's breath is sour or foul, health and fortune are likely to suffer…'"

"It sounds like some kind of manual for witch-doctors," Professor Guo complained.

"There's more," said Professor Xu after turning the page. "It has been claimed that birds, fish and animals use them as 'compasses', helping them find direction back to breeding grounds and to warmer climates during winter months. They have also been said to be vast prehistoric trade routes. It is believed that species as diverse as pigeons, whales, bees and even bacteria can navigate using the earth's magnetic field. It is thought that a tissue containing a substance called magnetite is responsible for this. Magnetite enables living creatures to sense magnetic changes and has been found in human tissue linked to the ethmoid bone in the front of the skull."

"Fascinating," declared Professor Guo barely suppressing a yawn. "What about the other book?"

"It's about the beliefs of the Australian Aboriginals," said Hu Ya opening it to what he hoped was a relevant section. He handed it to Professor Xu, whom he thought was more likely to take the information seriously.

"This looks interesting," he said and began to read from the book. "'The Rainbow Serpent is a great energy current that travels the world from Uluru (Ayers Rock) in central Australia, linking planetary increase sites or chakras, before meeting itself back in Uluru. The Australian Aborigines knew this serpent well. Their stories tell of two serpents; a female snake Kuniya and her nephew Liru, who meet at Uluru.'"

"More Stone Age nonsense," interrupted Professor Guo. "Does it say anything about pyramids?"

Professor Xu persevered. "'The Rainbow Serpent is the female aspect of two great energy lines. The other, the Plumed Serpent, is the male aspect. These serpents are themselves made up of male and female currents that intertwine like a Caduceus or Kundalini through the landscape.' This looks interesting," said Professor Xu sensing he was about to be interrupted again. "'The earthly representation of the planetary crown charka, which spreads out through the landscape zodiac, is Mt Kailash in Tibet!'"

"What's that supposed to mean?" asked Professor Guo.

"It lists the planetary Chakras," replied Professor Xu. "Here read it for yourself."

He handed the book to Professor Guo who read,

"'Crown Chakra – Mount Kailash, Tibet. Throat Chakra – Great Pyramid, Sphinx and Mount of Olives, Egypt. Heart Chakra – Glastonbury and Shaftesbury, England. Solar Plexus Chakra – Uluru, Australia. Sacral Chakra – Lake Titticaca, South America. Base Chakra – Mt Shasta, North America.'"

"Let's check these places on our map and see if they correspond to any of the pyramids," said Professor Xu as he and Hu Ya quickly located all the places listed. "There's a pyramid at every location! Look!"

"Ok, you've got me. That's pretty amazing," conceded Professor Guo.

"Pretty amazing? We've just confirmed a lot of what the artefact revealed from a completely independent source. This is utterly phenomenal!" exclaimed Professor Xu. He and Hu Ya embraced before indulging in some kind of pre-tribal ecstatic dance. Professor Guo continued to stare at the map, his smile growing exponentially.

"We've done it!" declared Professor Xu reaching for his trusty incineratives. "We've discovered something that is going to change not only the past but the entire future of the human race. This is the ultimate archaeological El Dorado!"

Hu Ya erupted in a yelp of excitement as Professor Guo joined the spontaneous dance of exhilaration which to an outside observer could probably best be compared to a chimpanzee mating frenzy.

"Is there any more?" asked Professor Guo.

"Let me take a look," said Professor Xu after igniting yet another cigarette. He retrieved the open book and began to read, "'Gaia's energy system is remarkably similar to our own. Our connection to the earth is also far greater than we realise, especially when the sixth planetary chakra or third eye, is held not in the landscape but in the consciousness of people. It moves with the precession of the equinoxes to a new location, which is currently in Avalon for the Age of Aquarius (Piscean Age – Jerusalem). We are the awareness of the planet. Her birthing pains are ours, and the plundering of her resources, we also feel as our own struggles.'"

"I don't think there's anything else relevant to Mt Kailash or sacred sights," said Hu Ya.

"Couldn't you find anything else specific to Mt Kailash?" complained Professor Xu.

"The government has censored most of the information about the Tibetan Plateau. It's considered too politically sensitive," said Hu Ya.

"But we're not interested in revolutions or anything political. Surely there must be some tourist information available," Professor Guo speculated. "Why don't you go to a travel agent and see if they've got anything?"

"Good idea," concurred Professor Xu, flicking through the rest of the book but failing to find any other relevant information.

160

EIGHTEEN - THE LECTURE

Meanwhile, many kilometres away on a rough country road, the minibus was nearing its destination. The driver hadn't slept and was almost at the limit of his ability to stay awake. The others were also weary, having only stopped twice for food and the other necessities their bodies demanded.

Irfan hadn't been able to completely bury Ping and Tashi's conversation in prayer. Amongst the thousands of words he couldn't understand, the words 'Mt Kailash' resonated like an interruption between himself and Allah. He'd regularly transported heroin past the impressive peak, in the employ of Dan Ban Ho. Eventually his curiosity got the better of him after the two words had been uttered several times in as many sentences.

"Mt Kailash," he said simply nodding his head at the other two passengers.

"Mt Kailash?" repeated Ping.

"You know Mt Kailash?" asked Tashi in Tibetan.

"Mt Kailash near my home," said Irfan innocently.

"Your home?" repeated Tashi incredulously.

Irfan nodded and smiled.

"What can you tell us about Mt Kailash?" asked Tashi.

That was a little too complicated for Irfan to comprehend so he repeated "Mt Kailash my home."

"What is it like?" attempted Tashi, using the simplest mono-syllabic words he could conjure.

"Very cold," replied Irfan.

Tashi laughed.

* * *

Professors Guo and Xu were both in a state of ecstatic amazement.

Again the door displayed its amazing propensity for being knocked.

"That was quick," said Professor Xu expecting Hu Ya.

The opened door revealed Professor Guo's exasperated secretary.

"You missed your first lecture," she accused. "You have another one in 10 minutes in lecture theatre four."

"Lectures?" In his excitement, the professor had completely forgotten the primary reason for his being at an institute of higher learning. He was a lecturer.

"You have a second year 'Methodologies in Archaeological Research' lecture scheduled. Do you want me to cancel it?"

"No. That won't be necessary. I'm sorry, I've been distracted. Thank you for reminding me."

She left without further comment.

"I'd better go," said Professor Guo.

"I'll be here when you get back," said Professor Xu.

Professor Guo strode purposefully from his office. He didn't have any notes. Today, for the first time in his career, he felt truly inspired.

He marched into Lecture Theatre Four like a Roman Emperor entering the Forum. Two hundred students immediately ceased conversing, opened their books and raised their pens in synchronised expectation.

"Good morning," began the professor.

"Today's lecture is about the inherent uselessness of a modern education. Nothing you have been taught in this or any other modern educational institution is of any real value. Our society prides itself on imagining that we are the most evolved and advanced humans in history. This is non-sense. You are all being desensitised to reality which is being systematically replaced by a vast, complex edifice of lies and misinformation. As individuals we have no power outside the construct in which we dwell. And it's not as if some imaginary super beings are controlling all this. The entire edifice has no controlling intelligence and has no real purpose other than to maintain the illusion within which we are all caught. Our thinking has become corrupted, and we have allowed it to happen.

"Other civilisations have existed on this planet with a far more healthy and worthwhile vision of what they were here for. We aren't even here for ourselves. Institutions like this university enable us to blend into what has become a form of planetary cancer. By numbing us to the consideration of other possibilities, modern education imposes a world view that is based entirely on the notion of exploitation. We are taught to exploit the education system for our own advantage without realising there is no ultimate advantage in any form of exploitation. We fail to notice ourselves discarding whatever real value our lives may once have had. We are tricked into becoming exploiters ourselves.

"Everybody knows about the phenomenon known colloquially as 'the naked official'. These corrupt pillars of our rotting society and declining values, steal everything they can and use the proceeds to send their families overseas, where they buy lavish houses and their children attend expensive schools. All in our name, all under the pretence that they are working for the greater good.

"They have exploited their positions of power to such an extreme degree they know that inevitably, one day they will be discovered. These people have already created escape routes for themselves once their crimes are exposed. They have no fear of the law. As soon as they know they are being investigated they will be on the next plane to join their family in some luxurious foreign location, far from the reach of those they have been systematically robbing for years.

"I'm not only speaking about our Chinese communist system. The west, if anything, is worse. It's like having a big brother who is a drug addict constantly borrowing and stealing from us while claiming to be setting a good example that we should follow. We've been bullied into following this disgraceful example and we have embraced the rot like children being given sweet poisons as an enticement to shamelessly pull our pants down for its petty amusement."

Most of the students had put down their pens and were staring in confused fear at a professor they assumed had gone mad. They'd never heard anybody dare to speak with such withering contempt.

Barely noticing the reaction of his students Professor Guo continued: "Education should be a process of opening young minds. It should instil ideals and encourage ideas to flourish. What do we do instead? We raise you to the point where you become sceptical of anybody who claims to have answers to any of the big questions in life. You come to believe that there is no ultimate authority you can turn to that can impart wisdom. The best we can do is to invalidate your questions and impose our own so that you lose sight of whatever it was that you were hoping to learn. And having imposed this ultimate form of confusion we tell you that now you know.

"When all you know is that you don't know, you become fit to graduate from this empty hall of crass stupidity. You are, in your own minds, experts, possessors of wisdom. In reality you are nothing but educated fools. You go out into the world and exploit it for everything you can. You believe you've earned this right to take your rightful place amongst the social elites, and are fit to carry forward mankind's sorry legacy.

"So where is wisdom? Where does it hide? Not within the walls of this institution. Nor is it out on the streets plying an honest trade in the service of its neighbours. It has been locked away in a secure dungeon, silenced and ridiculed, humiliated and despised, misrepresented and impersonated by fools. We have turned wisdom into a victim, but in the process we are the real victims. We are the ones who have to live an empty, shallow existence starved of any real intellectual sustenance, surrounded by other victims with whom we compete for the few trinkets we can recognise as valuable, in our degraded state."

Shocked by the professor's rant, students began to leave through the back doors of the lecture theatre.

Unperturbed, Professor Guo continued: "So much potential, so much beauty and truth have been squandered. The unjust thrive while the rest pray to some vaguely defined ideal, serve the Party or are simply too exhausted or deluded to care.

"The picture I am painting is bleak. That is true. What can be done about it? Are we doomed to watch our lives being devalued by the very fact that we are alive? We all have to eat, we need somewhere to live. There seems to be no way out except death.

"This is the reality we have created for ourselves. Nobody is to blame. It took many, many generations to arrive at this point. Many generations of good, caring people trying to create a better future for their children and this is where we are. Why does it have to be this way, those amongst you who can still think, must occasionally ask?

"It doesn't have to be this way. We are human beings with the potential to change everything but the change must begin inside our own heart. We must renounce exploitation, stop it dead.

"And then what? Every time we eat we must exploit some animal or plant. If we don't exploit what is in front of us then somebody else will and we will miss out. If we don't take our place in the race, we will lose. We will be left behind choking on the dust of the victors.

"The answer is empowerment. If we can turn away from exploitation and embrace empowerment we can seize back hope. We can change the world. So what is this magical ideal, empowerment? How do we empower instead of exploit? We simply have to stop being so selfish. If we can put others needs before our own and everyone does this, then we can empower each other. All we have to do is ask ourselves one simple question before we do anything. Is this exploiting somebody or something or is this empowering somebody or something? If the answer is exploitation, stop. Don't do it. If it is empowering then it is the right thing to do. It's that simple. We can turn this whole world around and create hope for each other."

A few of the students were quietly laughing. It appeared the professor had lost his mind.

"You can laugh," the professor continued. "Or you can listen and see another possibility. You are young, the future is yours. For some of you this idea of empowerment is nothing but a foolish old man's fantasy. You can't see outside the trap you are in. Some of you even imagine you like the trap. You'll be all right. You will be the exploiters so your future is going to be good. Why should anybody try to change anything?"

At that moment something unprecedented happened. One of the students threw an apple. It missed the professor and bounced off the blackboard behind him. For a few seconds time appeared to stand still. Nobody moved, nothing was said.

"Class dismissed," announced Professor Guo.

He left the lecture theatre like a wounded gladiator. They hadn't seen what he'd seen. They couldn't understand what he was saying. He wasn't going to change the world with one lecture. He wondered if he'd made one student think differently even for a moment as he made his way dejectedly back to his make-shift office.

He hoped he could rediscover the optimism he had felt before he'd entered the lecture theatre. Unfortunately this wasn't to be the case. Hu Ya had returned from several travel agents empty handed. He'd learnt that Mt Kailash was 1300 kilometres from Lhasa and though there was an airport in the vicinity, access to it was severely restricted. He wasn't able to secure anything pictorially. There were certainly no travel brochures and one travel agent had recommended he should visit Mt Everest instead.

* * *

When the call finally came through from Phuoc the next afternoon, Dan Ban Ho was beyond fury.

"Where the hell have you been?" he bellowed down the line.

Phuoc, hung over again, had only just woken up. The previous night he'd drunk two bottles of rice wine and had no recollection of anything after the first one. Fortunately he'd been too inebriated to commit any further atrocities. He had somehow managed to get himself back into his bed in the sub-budget hotel where he'd slept soundly until the afternoon sun roused him.

"The phone was out of order," he lied.

"Irfan has gone to the village of Womadige, near Nagqu in Tibet, with the two students. You will find them at the boy's parent's house. Leave immediately and don't fail me again! If you can't locate them, I have the girl's cell phone number. You are not to use it unless you have no alternative. Her name is Ping. Do you have a pen and paper?"

"Wait a moment, please." Phuoc approached the hotel's office and acting as politely as he was able, requested writing utensils. He returned to the phone and scribbled down the sequence of numbers Dan Ban Ho provided.

"I don't want him to get any closer to his home. Do not fail me again! Do you understand?"

The line went dead. Ho wasn't interested in the response. Phuoc had one last chance, otherwise the next assassin would have two targets. Life was cheap but death was even cheaper and there was no shortage of murderous thugs queuing up to get on Ho's payroll.

* * *

Tashi's parents were delighted when he and Ping finally arrived unannounced late in the afternoon. It had been a long journey and though it was infinitely more comfortable than the train, they were happy to get out of the minibus. The driver didn't bother to get out. As soon as they pulled up, he climbed into the back and went straight to sleep.

Belatedly Irfan clambered out of the minibus and tried to pretend he was invisible. That didn't work very well and after the usual barrage of kisses and hugs that included Ping and Tashi's father this time, Tashi introduced him to his parents.

They were led into the house. Free Chow waited impatiently for some attention, rubbing himself against Tashi's leg as Tashi's mother began the inevitable interrogation.

"Why didn't you tell us you were coming? We haven't got anything ready, and who's that man asleep in the van?"

"We left in a hurry," explained Tashi, finally picking up Free Chow.

"Are you in trouble?" asked Tashi's father.

"Not at all," said Ping reassuringly.

"The minibus belongs to the university," added Tashi. "They told us to come here so we wouldn't be followed by reporters. That thing Wen and I found up on the mountain is the Oracle of Singh Ma."

"The what?" asked Tashi's father.

"The Oracle of Singh Ma," repeated Ping merely reinforcing the aura of confusion that arrived with them.

"Sit here," said Tashi's mother, offering the hovering, uncertain Irfan a seat.

Irfan didn't understand and continued to hover in a state of confusion.

Ping took his hand and led him to a chair in front of the fire before planting herself down beside Tashi's father.

"Does everybody want tea?" asked Tashi's mother, attempting to restore normality.

"What is the Oracle of Singh Ha?" asked Tashi's father as he reached for his pipe.

"It's the Oracle of Singh Ma," corrected Ping.

"It's an ancient time capsule with a message from the past," Tashi attempted to explain. He wasn't entirely convinced that what he was saying was true but he knew that Ping's limited grasp of Tibetan would be even less helpful.

Tashi's mother fired a confused look at his father before disappearing into the kitchen to deal with things she understood.

"We have to go to Mt Kailash," announced Tashi effectively ending his parent's participation in the rest of the conversation.

"Mt Kailash," repeated Irfan attempting a smile and nodding his head, having finally understood something.

"Mt Kailash?" repeated Tashi's father, shaking his head in the absolute certainty that he understood nothing.

"It's a long story," said Tashi realising that even though they spoke the same language, his parents had even less hope of any understanding than Irfan.

"Mt Kailash is in Western Tibet," said Tashi.

"Why do you want to go to Western Tibet?" asked Tashi's mother from the kitchen.

"It's a long story," repeated Tashi.

"Does it have anything to do with somebody's teeth?" asked his mother appearing with a fully laden tray.

Inexplicably imagining he'd finally understood something, Irfan nodded his head enthusiastically.

"No," said Tashi, introducing a whole new level of confusion. "It's about archaeology."

"I'm studying archaeology," Ping attempted to contribute. She could see that language wasn't the only contributor to the confusion and lapsed into silence, deciding the wind probably had more to add to the conversation than anything she or Tashi were ever going to be able to contribute.

Again Irfan nodded enthusiastically, as he was handed a cup of yak butter tea.

NINETEEN - ARREST

Phuoc punched the ATM after it informed him that Dan Ban Ho hadn't deposited any more funds into his account. The machine was one of the older models and had probably been assaulted before. The only damage was to Phuoc's fist. He emitted a series of curses that could have restarted the Vietnam War had anybody been listening. How was he supposed to travel all the way to Tibet on 437 Yuan? That wasn't even enough to pay for his hotel room.

He stomped away muttering every word that every Vietnamese mother forbids her children to even think. After a few paces the unwanted realisation that 437 Yuan was quite a lot better in his pocket than sitting in the bank reached the reptilic cluster that ruled his brain. He grunted something an intellectually disadvantaged pig might have appreciated before turning back and withdrawing the money. After he'd pocketed the too few notes he gave the machine another slap just to let it know he hadn't forgiven it and walked away.

He stepped out onto the road and into the path of an unfortunate student who was riding home from his day's lectures on his 50cc Jialing motorbike. Phuoc's uncharacteristically ineffectual fist was employed once again. This time its effect was brutal and the unsuspecting victim was launched sideways, landing on the road with a broken jaw. The riderless motorbike careened into a bank on the side of the road, where Phuoc immediately claimed it.

Several pedestrians and motorists witnessed the event and started yelling at him and one particularly foolish bystander even attempted to chase after him.

Phuoc didn't even bother to grace the mayhem he'd caused with a backward glance. The torrent of protests receded behind him as he opened the throttle. After a few wrong turns he found his way out of town and onto the main highway. He was soon hurtling through the countryside, much to the amusement of everybody else on the road as his hunched bulk dwarfed the screaming two-stroke, struggling valiantly to acquit itself to the extreme limit of the specifications claimed by its Chinese designer.

* * *

Professor Guo returned to the room he was renting, a five minute walk from the university campus. He was exhausted and felt as though his brain had been doing marathons inside his skull. He had barely closed the door behind himself when somebody who sounded like they didn't like doors, started knocking on it. It was a violent, unhappy knock, insistent and impatient, a knock that made the professor fear for his door's safety.

He opened the battered portal to confront two policemen. They pushed it aside and attached themselves uncompromisingly to his arms.

"Professor Guo?" demanded the first, less than friendly policeman.

"What do you think you're doing?" the confused educator demanded.

That was the end of the verbal exchange.

What followed lacked dignity. The professor was manhandled into the back seat of a waiting police car and driven directly to the police station. The driver refrained from using the siren but the red and blue lights illuminated the passing urban scenery, increasing his anxiety.

Professor Guo slouched across the back seat, terrified that one of his students or another faculty member might recognise him.

The car pulled up outside the police station with all of the screeching, seedy theatrics of a badly produced, D grade Bollywood movie.

Professor Guo was manually dragged up the four stairs that led to the door of the station and through the front office, to a smaller office behind. A senior police officer grunted at his two subordinates as the professor was roughly planted onto a chair in front of his desk.

"Professor Guo," accused the senior officer.

The professor hadn't seen any Bollywood movies but he was aware of the principles governing his predicament and nodded.

"Thirty-nine students who attended a lecture delivered by you this afternoon have complained to us that you attempted to undermine not only our government, the Communist Party and the ideals upon which this country was founded, but that you also encouraged them to abandon their education and conform to some anti-communist doctrine stating that their academic endeavours were a complete waste of time. Have you gone mad?"

Professor Guo momentarily considered the merits of a plea of insanity before answering quietly, "Are you sure they were referring to me?"

The senior policeman instantly shed the miniscule aspect of his demeanour that might have been misinterpreted as empathy and brought his fist crashing down amongst the papers littering his desk.

"Do you realise the seriousness of these charges? You are a senior university lecturer! These allegations brought against you amount to treason!"

"What exactly am I being accused of having said?" asked the professor, who despite the intimidating display wasn't quite ready to abandon the professorial status he had worked for so many years to establish.

The policeman fixed him with a stare, cultivated over many years of law enforcement to rot flesh. Without any diminishment of the intensity or direction of his stare, the senior policeman picked up a sheet of paper and began to read from it.

"'That our society is a form of cancer. That your students are being desensitised by a complex edifice of lies and misinformation. That our society is completely out of control. That we are all exploited and being trained to be exploiters in turn. That our lives have no value and we are doomed to watch our lives being devalued further by the very fact that we are alive.' Would you like me to continue? I have another three pages of similar quotations."

"That won't be necessary," replied the professor, doing his best to sound as unperturbed as his panicking mind would allow. "These comments are all taken out of context. I was merely challenging my students to think beyond their preconceived convictions."

He was instantly aware that he should have said 'preconceived ideas' and his use of the word 'convictions' was an echo of the inner terror he was so desperately trying to conceal. He continued, "I was hoping to inspire in them exactly the response I've just heard from you. Archaeology is not a literal science like chemistry or physics. Obviously some of my students misunderstood the point I was attempting to make."

"And what exactly was the point you were attempting to make, Professor?" sneered the policeman, throwing the papers back onto his desk.

"The point was simply that they will make far better Party members and be able to contribute more to society if they don't take themselves too seriously. There is more to life than what they are learning at university."

"Our society is a cancer," repeated the policeman calmly, as though he'd just entered the eye of a hurricane. He wasn't about to be tricked by some upstart, university type.

"I was challenging them to imagine alternatives, to be creative."

"You were spreading sedition, Professor. We have very specific laws against the ideas you were attempting to teach. Laws that could have you incarcerated for many years. Laws that could have you executed. Take him away!"

The two officers, who had remained standing behind the professor, once again attached themselves to his arms and escorted him out of the office, down a dimly lit corridor and into a dingy jail cell. The clang that resounded down the corridor as the cell door was closed behind him was even less compromising than the senior officer had been.

Professor Guo knew he was in serious trouble. Fancy arguments and academic logic were not going to save him this time. At that moment exploitation wasn't even a small part of the mess he was in.

* * *

Anybody trying to follow Phuoc would merely have needed to follow the plume of blue/grey smoke trailing behind the Jialing as its 50cc, two stroke engine screamed its obvious distress at the disinterested sheep and yaks scattered across the slowly ascending plains. As he gained altitude the air became thinner and the temperature nose-dived. Cold wasn't one of the privations that life in tropical Vietnam had prepared him for. He was far more experienced at lacking food, friendship and fun than he was at lacking warmth.

Fortunately for Phuoc, the student had just filled the petrol tank before he'd been so callously ejected from his motorbike. But as night approached and the cold began to bare its blunt, brutal teeth, the needle on the petrol gauge plunged into the red just above the letter E.

Phuoc had no idea what the letter 'E' meant but he'd watched the gauge move purposely towards it for long enough to know that he didn't want the needle and the letter to effect their rapidly approaching rendezvous.

Assassins don't generally allow themselves to be thwarted by mundane inconveniences like running out of petrol and Phuoc had no intention of failing to conform with such a hallowed tradition. A lone farmer, returning to his village on a tractor towing a trailer load of hay, appeared in front of him on the otherwise deserted country road.

After he had bashed the farmer senseless, Phuoc briefly considered swapping the noisy uncomfortable two wheeled vehicle for the more ponderous tractor. But finding a piece of hose lying on top of the hay, practicality quickly overcame any thought of a more comfortable ride. After he filled the Jialing's almost empty tank, he continued his slow climb through the mountains.

The night grew darker and colder. The motorbike had a light but no means of providing any heat. Exhausted from his long day of theft and violence, he rode off the road and lay the bike down on its side behind a conveniently placed mud brick wall, positioning the Jialing's over heated engine in an attempt to provide himself with some warmth.

After less than an hour the motorbike was as cold as he was. Phuoc pushed it away and got up, shivering. This proved an even worse idea because the wall had been sheltering him from a snow-chilled wind.

Then, from about 50 metres away, he heard the unmistakable sound of a copper bell, the type local farmers attached to their yaks.

He followed the sound until he could see the outline of several of the hairy beasts standing in a group to protect themselves from the cold. He produced his trusty knife from his jacket pocket and lunged.

The yak's blood was warm as it drained from the throat of the closest beast. The rest of the herd dispersed in every direction as Phuoc thrust his blade into the belly of the dying animal. Warm offal spilled onto the cold earth. The stench was almost as debilitating as the cold.

Phuoc dragged the dead beast back to the mud brick wall and with the precision of a sushi chef hacked away most of the flesh and carved the warm remainder into a yak duvet. Dead flesh proved far more efficient than dead metal at keeping the cold away from his exhausted bones and he was soon snoring as contentedly as any yak.

He awoke just as the sun cast its first life affirming tentacles between the mountain peaks. Phuoc threw aside the now stinking remnants of the yak carcass and hauled himself to his feet. The motorbike lay on its side nearby. Within minutes he'd kicked it over enough times for it to be sucking in the mountain air and adding its smoke to the otherwise pristine environment.

Phuoc, covered in dried yak blood, unwashed, unfed and utterly uncouth, pointed the tortured two stroke towards the nearby road, released the clutch and resumed his morbid mission. He was determined that everything he confronted that day would suffer more than he had.

* * *

Despite his exhaustion Professor Guo didn't sleep well. About two and a half hours after he'd been thrown into the cell, the door was unlocked and a loudly protesting drunk was manhandled inside. He stood at the cell door for almost an hour declaring his innocence before he eventually gave up and turned his attention to the professor.

Professor Guo had never shared a room with anybody. China's one child policy had denied him any siblings. The nearest he'd been to an individual of the ilk he was now forced to deal with was possibly to pass them by walking down the street. Normally he would have crossed to the other side of the road to avoid such a person.

The drunk reeked of stale urine and looked as though he'd just been harvested from a field of potatoes. He ranted at the professor in some kind of street dialect that involved a lot of spit and cursing. The general thrust of his garbled diatribe was that he'd done nothing wrong and had left half a bottle of whiskey near where he'd been arrested for absolutely no reason whatsoever. The man was worried the whiskey had probably already been stolen and consumed by some real criminals whom the police had completely ignored.

Eventually he passed out, only occasionally mumbling a slurred defence of his innocence in between snores.

The next morning the professor was surprised to discover he'd managed to finally get some sleep, when he was rudely awakened by a grumbling policeman and the indescribably welcome arrival of Professor Xu. The drunk was still snoring loudly on the other bunk, having spent the night marinating in his own urine.

"Get me out of here!" Professor Guo implored.

"It's not going to be that easy," replied Professor Xu through the bars of the cell door. "I rang Party Secretary Guan as soon as I heard you'd been arrested and he's doing everything he can to help, but what did you tell your students yesterday?"

"I was just trying to pass on some of the information from the translation. I realise now I went too far and said a lot of things I shouldn't have said. I was utterly disoriented and should have cancelled the lecture."

"Disoriented? I've read the notes from one of your students. What possessed you to make such politically dangerous statements? You even talked about naked officials. How can you expect anybody to help you after you exposed them in a lecture to your students? You're being accused of counter-revolution."

"I was over-excited. I don't know. I wasn't trying to overthrow the Communist Party. The information in the translation was so incredible, I forgot everything else."

"I agree, it was mind boggling. Just try to relax. I'm doing everything I can to get you out of here. Hopefully the Party Secretary will be able to sort this out, but until he does, I'm afraid you're just going to have to try and be patient."

At that moment the drunk woke up and leapt off the bunk as if he'd just been electrocuted.

"Where am I?" he bellowed. "Who stole my whiskey? If you don't give it back, I'll kill you all."

"Help!" screamed Professor Guo.

"Guards!" screamed Professor Xu.

By the time a guard finally unlocked the cell door, Professor Guo was being strangled.

The sound of a wooden baton connecting with an unprotected human head is never pleasant. However on this occasion the two professors were both extremely grateful to hear it. Blood splattered across Professor Guo's terrified face as his cell mate released his murderous grip and slumped forward, back into the waiting vortex of unconsciousness.

TWENTY - UNRELENTING EVIL

By evening, every muscle, every sinew and every other part of Phuoc with a nerve attached to it, was adding its note of tortured agony to the Jialing's wailing scream as it continued to haul his malevolent form onward and upward. He had refilled the petrol tank twice during the day. Once at the expense of another unwary farmer and once at a petrol station in Golmud where he actually paid for it, using all the money he'd taken from the farmer and a few Yuan of his own.

With the Jialing refuelled he decided to take pity on his own empty gut and invested some of his meagre funds in a packet of dried fruit before resuming his journey.

Phuoc rode until the sun set behind the snow covered peaks which now had him surrounded. It was worse than bitterly cold. His hands were frozen to the motorbike's handlebars as he spotted a small mud brick building less than 50 metres from the road.

Without bothering to consult with his brain, his arms automatically steered the bike towards the primitive structure. Some god who liked evil, murderous thugs, had left some patties of yak dung mixed with straw in the corner of the abandoned structure. He was able to start a small fire and its warmth infused his aching, freezing bones.

Sleep was almost instantaneous.

He awoke several times in the night, colder than he'd imagined life could endure. He poked at the embers of the fire and was able to convince it to produce a little more anti-cold. The wind, fresh from the freezing snows of the mountain peaks, ensured that heat wasn't an option. Mother nature herself shivered uncontrollably, prowling outside on the desolate landscape.

Once again the sunrise heralded his final unappealable awakening and after he'd warmed himself by several minutes of attempting to kick over the extremely reluctant Jialing, he was back out on the road.

He reached Nagqu by mid-morning and turned off the main road. There were no sign posts and it seemed as if everything had been placed especially to annoy him. He'd managed to glance at a map at the petrol station the day before and had a vague notion of where he was going. Within half an hour he'd navigated the rough track that took him to Womadige.

He abandoned the Jialing on the side of the track and walked the last 100 metres to the scattering of houses.

During the two and a half days of solitary riding it had taken him to get there, he hadn't bothered to formulate any kind of plan. Then suddenly the same god who'd placed the yak patties and straw for him the previous night led him to notice the relatively fresh tire tracks left by the university minibus. The tracks were the only trail left in the mud by anything other than a tractor or an animal. It was obvious the minibus had been driven off the track and spent some time parked outside one of the houses.

As he approached the house his mind finally engaged. By the time he knocked on the wooden door he had devised a strategy which he hoped would get him past it.

Tashi's mother opened her front door and was confronted by a filthy, stinking man, covered in dried blood and straw. He spoke Chinese with a thick accent. He pointed at the track and uttered Ping's name. After the strange events of the last few days, Tashi's mother accepted that he must be somebody else from the university and invited him inside.

"You look like you need to wash," she observed gesturing for him to sit down in the kitchen by the warm stove.

Over a cup of hot yak butter tea, she tried to explain that Tashi, Ping and their other friend had left the previous day to drive to Mt Kailash.

Phuoc understood nothing. It didn't take long before he tired of her noisy antics and unable to contain his rage, spilt his tea, cursing loudly in some language she'd never heard before. Excusing herself on the pretext of checking on the water, she escaped into an adjoining bedroom and called through the window to her husband, who was outside tending the vegetable garden. He could hear the fear in his wife's voice and dropped the hoe he was working with, quickly entering the house through the back door.

Tashi's mother gestured him to silence as he began to ask her what was wrong. She merely pointed in Phuoc's direction, her expression conveying mute distress.

Tashi's father walked into the kitchen to confront the filthy stranger's malevolence.

"Who are you!" he demanded to know.

Phuoc didn't bother to answer. He launched himself at Tashi's father and within less than one second the old man's blood was staining the dirt floor.

Phuoc didn't wait for Tashi's mother to reappear. He was in the bedroom with his blood soaked knife smearing her husband's fresh blood across her otherwise spotless dress before Free Chow had even smelt it in the cold mountain air.

"What are you doing?" she screamed.

"Shut up!" he commanded, shoving her backwards so she fell onto the floor. Tashi's mother began to call her husband's name in between sobs. Phuoc kicked her in the stomach.

"Shut up!" he repeated un-phased by the fact that she obviously had no conception of what he was demanding.

She began to sob hysterically.

"Shut up!" Phuoc commanded for the third time, administering another vicious kick to her stomach. This time Tashi's mother responded by vomiting.

Phuoc grabbed a handful of hair, dragging the distraught old woman to her feet.

Looking around the bedroom he found some twine used for bundling vegetables and used it to tie the still sobbing woman's hands behind her back. Then he tied her to the bed and returned to the kitchen. Stepping over Tashi's father's dead body he began ransacking the kitchen for food. He found some rtsam-pa, barley flour mixed with yak's milk, which he noisily devoured.

There was a pot of water Tashi's mother had placed on the stove to heat for him to have a much needed wash. It was steaming by now and he ripped off most of his filthy rags, before using the warm water to disperse the fresh blood, dried blood, yak offal and general filth coating his arms and body. Some of Tashi's father's clothes were drying by the fire and he selected a few of the drier items. Fortunately for him Tibetans tend to wear ill fitting, baggy clothes and he managed to find enough pieces to dress himself.

He returned to the bedroom feeling and smelling considerably fresher. This failed to impress Tashi's mother, whose eyes were flashing raw terror.

"Telephone!" he demanded at Tashi's mother who understood the universally used word and shook her head.

"Nagqu," she sobbed quietly, terrified at how he might respond.

Phuoc produced his cell phone. Lacking other options he hoped this was the type of circumstance his distant employer would approve of. He untied Tashi's mother's hands, dialled the number he had scrawled on a piece of paper in his pocket and handed her the phone.

She took the phone in her trembling hands, hoping it wouldn't ring. It did.

Meanwhile, in Lhasa events were not unfolding in any predictable way. Ping had never been to the ancient capital city of Tibet before. She was unprepared for the tragic majesty of the city itself. She was struck by the empty presence of the Potala palace, once the home of the Dalai Lamas. The quiet despondency she sensed in the Tibetans as they went about their daily business, never making eye contact or smiling like their rural brethren made her sad.

Parts of the city of Lhasa were like the abandoned sets of a war movie. The cold mountain air whistled past barricades sparsely patrolled by soldiers wielding weapons, too real for them to qualify as actors.

Irfan was first to notice the disturbance. He didn't understand why they had stopped to be tourists in Lhasa and was reluctantly following Tashi, Ping and the driver through over-policed streets to some unknown destination for some no doubt un-fathomable purpose.

The disturbance grew louder until it literally ignited. Ten metres to their left two young monks chose that precise moment to immolate. Irfan was sure he recognised one of them as the young tulku whose procession he'd hitched a ride with before the police shot him.

Everyone stopped. Everything except the grotesquely crackling fire stopped. The street was filled with the sweet stench of burning flesh.

Then in a torrent, suddenly there was movement and noise. People started yelling and running around. Somebody began to wail. The two flaming bodies were still as the flames crackled and spat, a last gesture of futile defiance.

One of the bodies fell onto its side. Ping could see its teeth as the flames slowly erased the still proud face.

Tashi was horrified. He'd never seen an immolation before. He'd heard they happened but hadn't previously considered the gruesome reality of such a spectacle. The pain must have been excruciating! Who could bare so much agony and why would anybody choose to die that way? Tashi had witnessed death before. He'd seen several of the older villagers after they'd died but watching people actually die, was very different. Especially considering they had chosen to do this of their own free will. All the pain and the loss were a result of premeditated choice.

How could anybody's life get to that point?

The young tulku had been captured by the Chinese after most of the monks protecting him were either dead or in jail. He was given an ultimatum by the Chinese authorities. He either spread communist party propaganda and denied his Buddhist destiny, or he went to jail to be tortured for the rest of his life. As far as the Chinese were concerned the choice was simple. They had failed to perceive the third option, that self preservation was not his major priority.

The seven year old tulku had spent a lot of his short life meditating on impermanence. He already knew that life is impermanent and so is death.

The Buddha taught that if one cannot help others, one should refrain from harming them. If he allowed the Chinese to use his position to spread ignorance and superstition, he would be causing a lot of harm and this would result in suffering.

This incarnation had been unfortunate. His only option as a bodhisattva committed to relieving the suffering of others was to remove himself so that he couldn't be used to cause others to suffer. If he was unable to teach the Buddha's Dharma then he should seek a more favourable rebirth.

His 11-year-old retainer agreed. He didn't want to live like a slave in a prison. He had already been beaten and tortured in a futile attempt to gain information about his master's whereabouts during the weeks before his capture. He'd been tortured enough to understand that they were up against something so hard and so unflinchingly cold, it would never conceive the beauty and freedom offered by the Dharma.

They had soaked their maroon monk's robes in petrol overnight, sequestering the fuel from the seldom used, lonely monastery generator. The smell was suffocating as they made their way to the square in front of the Potala Palace. They each carried a litre bottle of fuel and were soon in position, having eluded the morning police patrols.

They sat down on the road and just as people began to realise what was about to happen, they poured petrol over themselves. The young tulku struck a match, and smiled at his retainer for the last time as a sheet of orange flame engulfed them both.

The two young monks both sat calmly. One of them appeared to show some pain for a few seconds but then regained his composure and relaxed quietly into his death. The other barely moved.

Ping's phone rang.

"Hello?" answered Ping. What else could she do?

Unable to respond verbally, Tashi's mother said nothing, punctuated by a few muffled sobs.

Phuoc wrenched the phone from her. "If you want to see her alive, meet me at the first tea house outside Nagqu on the way to Lhasa," he growled, aware that if he remained in the village, the discovery of Tashi's father's body could jeopardise his mission. He had noticed an old Soviet built car which looked like it still ran, parked beside one of the houses near where he'd abandoned the Jialing. It looked big enough to fit Tashi's mother in the trunk.

"Who is this?" demanded Tashi, glad of a distraction after Ping had turned white and mutely handed him her phone.

"If you want to see your mother again, alive, meet me at the first tea house outside Nagqu on the way to Lhasa. I will swap her for the Kashmiri, Irfan Mullaramzan. You have one hour."

For a moment there was silence. "We are in Lhasa," replied Tashi's trembling voice. "It will take us about three hours. Please don't hurt her," he begged. "Can I speak to her?" he implored as the line went dead.

* * *

Jose Liqualottapuss was a rugby union player. He had migrated from his native Chile in the hope of qualifying to play for the world's greatest rugby union team, the New Zealand All Blacks. Unfortunately, having no tangible connection to New Zealand other than his love of the game and its ultimate team, he was ineligible. However he was accepted to play regional rugby in New Zealand and after a series of false starts finally ended up playing for Waikato. After five years he was a household name, celebrated everywhere in what the locals referred to as 'the Waikato'. Jose had no problem with the 'the' because he doubted there were any other Waikato's anywhere else in the world and if it was the only Waikato then it was indubitably 'the Waikato'.

His girlfriend, Moana Jeffries was a New Zealand national and proudly claimed to be half Maori. She was a direct descendant of Hone Heke, a Maori warrior who had dared to chop down a flagpole which held aloft the hated Union Jack before the Treaty of Waitangi was signed between the indigenous Maori and the British.

The couple were holidaying in Tibet as Jose considered his future. In hindsight he would have been better off travelling to Argentina to play for the Puma's, now his dream of ever wearing an all black jersey had been finally and irrevocably denied.

Jose played in the position referred to as prop in the front row of the forward pack. He was five feet eleven inches tall and weighed 116 kilograms. Both on and off the rugby field he was formidable.

As he and Moana sat drinking the local yak butter tea, a minibus pulled up outside the Shengcan Baoxiang Restaurant. A lone Tibetan got out and strode inside as the minibus turned around taking its three remaining occupants back the way they had come.

Tashi was relieved to see that he had arrived before Phuoc. He had no idea how he was going to deal with the assassin face to face but at least they had some time to try and affect their hastily devised strategy. The only other people in the teahouse besides the owner and his daughter were a young foreign couple sitting together near the window. Tashi's mind was racing, his system flushed with adrenalin,

He and Ping had agreed that Tashi's mother's life was far more precious than her father's freedom, but even so, neither felt they could deliver Irfan into the cold blooded hands of somebody intent on his murder.

"Don't you know somebody with a gun?" Ping had asked as they sped along the highway towards their dreaded rendezvous.

"He's probably got one and probably knows how to use it," Tashi had replied.

Irfan sat silently praying to Allah. Though not entirely sure what was happening, he sensed it had something to do with him. The fear and panic that accompanied them back from Lhasa was in stark contrast to the excited, carefree journey they'd been enjoying before the immolation. The minibus pulled off the road half a kilometre from the restaurant. Its three occupants hastily made their way back to the restaurant. The desolate, treeless landscape provided no place to hide. Fortunately nobody was watching and they positioned themselves outside the restaurant, near a window that allowed them a limited view of its interior.

The two foreigners were engaged in an intense conversation in English. Nobody else understood a word they were saying.

* * *

The old Soviet car had been easy to hot wire and Tashi's mother fitted uncomfortably into its trunk. Most of the villagers were busy working in the fields and nobody noticed it being stolen. It had a few holes in its inefficient exhaust system which besides almost gassing both its occupants to death, announced their imminent arrival from quite a distance away.

The car's breaks badly needed new pads or even some lesser worn old ones. They proved to be more efficient at making noise than at stopping the vehicle, which finally came to a noisy halt as it collided with the front of the restaurant.

Phuoc's first interaction with Jose was to inadvertently spill his tea as the restaurant absorbed the last of the car's momentum.

Phuoc almost ripped the car's door from its hinges as he stepped out onto the gravel car park. He stomped into the restaurant.

Tashi recognised his father's clothes on the body of the malevolent mongrel advancing towards him.

"Where is he?" demanded Phuoc.

"Where's my mother?" countered Tashi rising to his feet.

Phuoc kicked the table away from between them and continued his advance. This constituted Phuoc's second unintentional interaction with Jose as most of the contents of a sugar bowl landed in his lap.

Jose had come to the Himalayas to experience peace and tranquillity. He might have been able to overlook his own spilt tea and the sugar but the fact that his girlfriend Moana was wearing most of her tea constituted a serious breach of etiquette.

The final spark that ignited the situation was the sudden appearance of Phuoc's knife.

Jose launched. Years of rugby training had produced an athlete who wasn't merely large and powerful, Jose was fast.

Before Phuoc had even recognised him as a threat, Jose's fist broke Phuoc's jaw in three places and gave Tashi an unforgettable demonstration of a very efficient alternative method of teeth extraction to those he'd been taught at dentistry school.

Phuoc, despite being airborne and badly injured wasn't ready to accept defeat. He landed, rolled and came up blade first, ready for round two.

The restaurateur, witnessing the destruction of some of his business's key assets, immediately called the police.

The minibus driver, Ping and Irfan ran into the restaurant and armed themselves with chairs. But their contribution was unnecessary.

Phuoc lunged. Jose affected a side step, his trademark move playing for the Waikato. The blade inflicted a shallow cut in his left bicep as Jose connected his right fist with the back of Phuoc's head and brought his left knee up into Phuoc's face. The manoeuvre was as graceful as it was effective. There was no round three.

Jose took possession of Phuoc's knife as the assassin lay unconscious on the blood splattered floor.

"If you ever spill my girlfriend's tea again, next time you make sure you say 'sorry'," said Jose, returning to Moana who tended his bleeding arm.

"The police are on their way," said the restaurateur from behind the locked kitchen door.

"Where's my mother?' repeated Tashi rolling the unconscious Phuoc onto his back and exposing the mess Jose had made of his face.

"Tie him up," demanded the minibus driver.

The restaurateur unlocked the kitchen door and emerged with some rope. Irfan and the driver soon had Phuoc securely trussed.

Tashi and Ping meanwhile, were out in the car park and soon had the trunk open after his mother recognised her son's voice and started yelling for help and pounding on its lid.

"Are you all right?" he asked, tears welling in his eyes at the sight of his badly beaten mother.

"I'm Ok," she replied as they attempted to lift her out.

"Argh!" she screamed in pain. "I think he broke my ribs."

"What about dad? Is he all right?" asked Tashi as he and Ping gently helped her to climb out.

"I don't know," his mother whimpered as they helped her into the minibus which the driver had retrieved from its hiding place.

"Take us to Nagqu People's Hospital," ordered Tashi. "I'll direct you when we get to town."

TWENTY ONE - CHINESE JUSTICE

Three hours later the police finally arrived at the restaurant.

Jose and Moana had already left.

Irfan remained and was armed with a heavy club the restaurateur had provided in case Phuoc regained consciousness.

Ping and Tashi had reluctantly returned from the hospital after Tashi's mother was admitted and it was obvious they could do no more than wait. Ping spent the trip back to the restaurant talking to Sun Xuefa, her father's lawyer, on her cellphone. She was less than impressed with Nagqu Hospital and instructed him to contact the hospital and ensure Tashi's mother received the best possible care they could provide.

Two Chinese policemen strode into the teahouse, which by now had been restored to its original condition.

"So what's the problem?" asked the older of the pair relaxing into a chair.

"This one came in here and started a fight with this one," reported the restaurateur, indicating the bleeding, trussed Phuoc and Tashi.

"It looks like he picked on the wrong person," laughed the older policeman accepting a cup of tea.

"No! Another customer did this to him and then left," explained the restaurateur. The younger policeman immediately arrested Irfan, handcuffing his hands behind his back.

"This man is an assassin," said Ping, indicating the immobilised Phuoc. "He kidnapped and beat up Tashi's mother and he was trying to kill the man you just arrested."

"Arrest them both," instructed the senior officer waving discursively at Phuoc and Irfan.

"Why are you arresting him?" asked Tashi pointing at Irfan.

"He's a wanted man. We have a picture of him at the police station. He's a member of a criminal gang."

"He was tried in Hong Kong and acquitted," said Ping.

"He's under arrest!" stated the senior policeman emphatically.

Irfan and Phuoc were taken outside and manhandled into the waiting police car.

"Don't put them in the same cell," Tashi almost pleaded. "The assassin will kill him."

"Nagqu police station is not a hotel," snapped the senior officer.

Ping approached the senior officer and handed him a wad of 100 Yuan notes.

"Don't lock them up together," she said as the senior officer flicked through the wad of cash before pocketing it.

"I'll see what I can do," he said, climbing into the police car and speeding away with lights flashing and siren blaring.

Nagqu police station was less like a hotel than a barn. It looked like it had been thrown together by a committee of drunks standing on the other side of the street. It only had one cell, which already held another occupant. Irfan and Phuoc were pushed and dragged inside. The cell door squealed on its rusting hinges.

"Mohamed!" exclaimed Irfan recognising the other prisoner.

"Irfan? I thought you were dead!"

"So did I," replied Irfan in Kashmiri as he embraced his old friend.

Mohamed had been one of the enforcers whose job was to escort the drug couriers through villages where they might otherwise have had to deal with the local thugs.

"Weren't you inside the cave when it was raided?"

"Yes, but I managed to escape."

"How?"

"I was lucky. But then I was arrested and taken to Hong Kong."

Sometime during their conversation, the small concentration of reptilic brain cells which controlled Phuoc's mind, attained consciousness. The first sensation they recorded was the pain emanating from everything above his shoulders. Then they became conscious of the cold, hard cell floor where he lay sprawled. Next they heard a conversation in a language he didn't recognise before his memory joined his expanding awareness, adding the realisation that he was on a mission to kill somebody. This realisation was augmented by the knowledge that it wasn't only his victim who was in mortal danger but that he would share a similar fate if he failed. A vague recollection of the events that transpired in the restaurant served to stir the small knot of reptilic brain cells to action.

Phuoc attempted to open his eyes. His left eye acquiesced but the other one was sealed shut with dried blood. His limited vision revealed the uncompromising interior of the jail cell. The only thing he could recognise was that his situation was not good.

Without moving he concentrated on the voices coming from behind him, slightly to his left. There were two, both males engaged in what sounded like a friendly, happy exchange. From this he deduced that anybody who was happy with him sprawled on the floor, damaged and in pain, definitely wasn't on his side.

He lay motionless, concentrating his depleted reserves for several minutes before he attacked.

He reared up like a cobra whose body hadn't quite been severed from its tail. In the blurry haze he recognised Irfan. Another positive.

Lacking weaponry, he launched himself at Irfan's throat. That was a tactical mistake. Exhaustion, a lack of nutrition and blood, combined with dizziness from having absorbed three good hits from Jose meant he was far less efficient as a killing machine than usual. It also meant both his hands were engaged in the undignified act of attempting to strangle Irfan.

Mohamed possessed two un-deployed paws and used one of them to swat Phuoc like an oversized, overly inconvenient fly.

"Who's this clown?" he asked almost casually as Phuoc's already battered skull collided with the cell floor.

"He works for Dan Ban Ho," gasped Irfan. "He's been trying to kill me for weeks."

Mohamed swung his boot and connected squarely with the already bloody wreckage of Phuoc's face. Then, as if Phuoc no longer existed, he and Irfan sat on the bed and continued to piece together an understanding of what had transpired since they last worked together transporting Dan Ban Ho's heroin.

Less than an hour later, an apologetic police officer unlocked the cell door and politely invited Irfan to accompany him to freedom.

"I'll get you out of here as soon as I can," said Irfan using Phuoc's back as a door mat and exiting the cell.

"I'm very sorry about the misunderstanding," said the policeman to Irfan.

Understanding nothing, Irfan smiled.

Tashi and Ping were waiting for him as he emerged from the cell block.

"My friend," said Irfan excitedly. This confused Ping who assumed Irfan had somehow made friends with the assassin.

"My friend, witness," elaborated Irfan pointing back towards the cell.

"A witness for what?" asked Tashi.

"Witness, father. Dan Ban Ho."

"Are you sure?" asked Tashi, unsure he was grasping the true meaning of Irfan's unusually succinct Tibetan.

"Yes. My friend, he know Dan Ban Ho."

"Does he mean what I think he means?" asked Ping.

Tashi translated into the simplest, mono-syllabic Tibetan he could muster. Irfan appeared to understand and nodded his head enthusiastically.

"My friend," Irfan attempted, gesturing happily towards the cell block. Tashi quickly erased Ping's confusion with a few sentences in Mandarin.

"Tell him about the call to my cell phone," said Ping. "Tell him my father's lawyer thinks he may be able to establish a link between the assassin and Dan Ban Ho."

"That might be pushing it a bit far," said Tashi. "It sounds like his friend in the cell knows about the heroin smugglers. If he's found another witness, we might have enough evidence to clear your father's name."

Tashi looked at Irfan. It required far too many complex words to explain.

"Mother?" asked Irfan.

"Hospital," answered Tashi. The word 'hospital' was several continents beyond Irfan's linguistic borders. "She's Ok," Tashi qualified.

Irfan nodded.

"My friend," said Irfan his voice laced with concern. The concern was mistakenly assumed by both Tashi and Ping to mean Irfan wanted them to get Mohamed out of jail. What it actually meant was that Irfan was worried Mohamed might kill Phuoc if they remained in the same cell. Irfan wasn't worried about Phuoc's welfare. He was worried that Mohamed might be charged with murder, an outcome that wouldn't be helpful to anybody's cause.

"The lawyer will be here in the morning," said Tashi. "He will fix everything."

"Killer, big danger," insisted Irfan.

Ping looked at Tashi. They had both understood Irfan's words but the meaning eluded them.

"Let's go home," said Tashi oblivious to the horror that awaited them.

* * *

Professor Guo had vainly hoped his removal from the cell he'd been forced to share with several common criminals, signalled he was about to be granted his freedom. For a few priceless minutes relief and happiness flooded into his sadly deluded mind. In reality, he was being transferred from Weicheng Prison in Xi'anyang to a larger, more modern facility in Xi'an. After a half hour journey in the back of a prison van, he was escorted into the larger, more impregnable concrete complex and deposited in another cell which housed another seven inmates.

After a further two days haunted by humiliation and fear, his hopes were again raised as he was roughly escorted out of the cell, but this time he was led into a visiting room. Professor Xu was waiting for him behind a set of extremely intimidating bars and a window constructed from bullet proof glass. Despite this being one of the rare occasions when he wasn't smoking a cigarette, Professor Xu looked even less healthy than usual. He appeared to have aged another decade since their last meeting.

From his appearance it seemed things weren't going any better on the outside.

Professor Guo fumbled meekly with the telephone handset indicated by a burly prison guard as Professor Xu spoke softly into a corresponding piece of apparatus on the other side of the barrier separating them.

"How are you?" asked Professor Xu, as if the answer wasn't blindingly obvious.

"When can you get me out of here?" blurted Professor Guo.

There was an ugly pause before Professor Xu answered. "That's not going to be so easy."

"What do you mean?"

"I mean you are in very serious trouble."

"What about Party Secretary Guan? I thought you said he was going to help."

"He did everything he could, but he has to be careful. The police raided the university. They confiscated the artefact and seized all the recordings we made when we unlocked its message."

Professor Guo's hand began to tremble as he held the receiver to his shocked head.

"They've decreed the artefact to be subversive. They said its message is counter-revolutionary," continued Professor Xu. "They raided my home and warned me not to continue to investigate anything connected with the artefact otherwise I'll end up on the other side of this barrier with you."

Professor Guo started to cry.

"I'm sorry," attempted Professor Xu, finally relenting and removing a cigarette packet from his pocket. "The notes from your lecture have been given to the Central Committee. Nobody connected with this situation is safe. The entire Archaeology Department has been suspended. All our activities have been cancelled pending an investigation."

* * *

In Tibet, the situation was even worse. Tashi, Ping and Irfan returned to Tashi's parent's house in Womadige. The driver stayed in the minibus after indicating he was happy to spend another night inside the vehicle.

The village was shivering in the shadow of Mt Luguna as Tashi lit a yak butter lamp and called out to his father. An unexpected silence emanated from the cold, dark interior. The fire in the kitchen had stopped burning for the first time in decades.

Ping lit another lamp as they advanced inside, confusion masking the unspoken fear percolating between them. Irfan could also sense that something was wrong and waited near the front door.

Ping found the body. She pushed open the kitchen door as Tashi checked his parent's bedroom.

In the flickering light of the lamp, the large lump lying on the floor in the centre of the room looked like a pile of dirty washing. Ping approached it and then recognised Tashi's father's face protruding from the inert pile.

She screamed.

Tashi was at her side within seconds, and then he too realised that the unusual mound was in fact a body.

Irfan heard Ping's scream, but lacking a light, he tripped over a chair and landed on the floor as Tashi emitted a wail of heart wrenching despair. Irfan managed to get to his feet and reached the doorway. Illuminated by the glow from the two yak butter lamps, he could see Ping frozen in horror as Tashi attempted to elicit some signs of life from his father's blood soaked corpse.

Within minutes several neighbours had joined the driver at the front door. More lamps were lit and soon the full reality of the tragedy was exposed for all to see.

Tashi sobbed uncontrollably as he held his father's cold body in his arms.

By now, half the people of the village were inside the house, adding confusion to the miserable scene.

* * *

Eventually the sun rose. A cock crowed as the village of Womadige attempted to absorb the events of the previous day.

Tashi and Ping had spent the night together in the same bed for the first time, comforting each other.

Grief had overwhelmed the entire village and they lay at its focal point. Neither slept.

The monks arrived early, summoned to perform the last rites according to the Tibetan Book of the Dead.

Half mad with grief and lack of sleep, Tashi met them at the front door and told them to take their stone age superstition away. He considered the notion of reading to the dead, primitive and ignorant. All the traditional Buddhist practices revolted him, especially sky burial, where they hacked the corpse to pieces and flung it to the four cardinal directions to feed the vultures.

It was Ping who reasoned that this would be what both his parents wanted and expected to happen. She gently urged Tashi to reconsider by pointing out that failure to adhere to tradition would cause his injured mother further unnecessary distress. She opened the door to admit the four monks when he finally relented. They had begun their ceremony outside the house and were already burning incense and chanting as they entered.

Shortly afterwards, a private jet landed at Lhasa airport and disgorged a be-suited Hong Kong lawyer. Sun Xuefa wasted no time and by midday the first black Mercedes ever to enter Womadige pulled up outside the house.

By now the village was awash with rumours and accusations regarding Tashi's ill-considered romantic entanglement with a rich Chinese girl. The sight of the black Mercedes pulling up beside the university minibus and the immediate admission of a Chinaman in a suit was enough to convince most of the villagers that they were being invaded. The fact that the monks were made to wait outside the house for almost half an hour, an ultimate display of disrespect, only served to attenuate the innuendo.

After another half hour, Tashi, Ping, Irfan and the be-suited Chinaman re-emerged and disappeared into the Mercedes which then bumped and rattled out towards the main highway.

Tashi entered the ward where his mother was being treated, alone. His mother was happy to see him and was sitting up in bed watching one of the few television sets she had ever seen.

194

Her happiness faded quickly. Even through the delirium of painkillers she could tell by her son's demeanour something even worse had happened.

"Father is dead," was all Tashi could manage to say before a group of nurses whisked her out of the crowded public ward, down a bleach smelling corridor and into a private room. Tashi followed like a wounded puppy. After a few minutes of taking her temperature and fussing over her pillows, the nurses left her and Tashi alone.

His mother stared at her son through wide, disbelieving eyes. He took her in his arms and they both wept.

Meanwhile, Ping and Irfan sat silently in the Mercedes.

Sun Xuefa spent the time on his cell phone organising a medivac helicopter to fly Tashi's mother to the best hospital in Hong Kong.

POSTLUDE

The retrial of Ping's father took only two days to acquit him and set him free. Irfan and Mohamed provided compelling testimony that linked Dan Ban Ho to enough of his crimes to have an international arrest warrant issued and Interpol alerted to track him down. He was never found.

Phuoc failed to rouse from the cell floor a second time and survived the night. He was eventually taken, under heavy police guard to the Nagqu People's Hospital where he recovered from his injuries. Ping's cell phone records and several eyewitnesses guaranteed that this was his last ever experience outside a maximum security jail.

Irfan received a two year suspended sentence, due to his cooperation and returned home to his family in Kashmir with enough of Ping's father's money to never have to transport heroin again.

Mohamed also received a suspended sentence but was back inside prison within six months on unrelated charges.

Ping and Tashi were married the following year. They never returned to Xian'yang and Tashi transferred to a dental school in Hong Kong, where he graduated the following year. Ping gave birth to a baby boy they named Yucai and became a full time mother while Tashi was set up in business by Ping's father and spent the rest of his life pulling out teeth and inserting fillings.

Tashi's mother recovered from her injuries and despite the protests of her son and Ping's family, she returned to Womadige where she lived out the rest of her days in relative luxury, purchasing a new house paid for by Ping's family.

Professor Guo's widowed mother received an official letter from the Central Communist Government in Beijing. It required her to reimburse them for the cost of a bullet. The bullet had been fired into the back of her son's head early one morning in a field outside the thriving city of Xi'an. Three months later she died of a broken heart.

Hu Ya failed his way out of university and moved south to Chengdu. He eventually accepted employment as a street cleaner and married a traffic warden. They produced a daughter whom they named Dierdre.

The Oracle of Singh Ma was never officially seen again. Several attempts to destroy it failed and it was eventually included as land-fill beneath a sixty story building somewhere in south-eastern China. No official records pertaining to its fate were kept.

Professor Xu was paid a substantial amount by Party Secretary Guan in return for a promise never to mention the Oracle again. The money enabled him to retire, divorce his wife and move to France where he lives a secluded life in a vineyard near Bordeaux.

Occasionally, after a few glasses of Beaujolais and a packet of Gitanes, he tells improbable stories to the few disbelieving locals able to extract meaning from his peculiar mixture of French and Mandarin. He is generally considered a lovable eccentric with an over active imagination and too much time on his hands. If anyone 'does manage to follow his animated rants about a fantastic discovery he was once involved with back in his days as an archaeologist in China, the members of his audience smile knowingly and affectionately pour him another glass of wine.

THE END

www.ianpurdie.com